# BELIEVING AGAIN:
# A TALE OF TWO CHRISTMASES

**Martin Crosbie**

*For my children,*
*Andrew, Giada, and Cassidy,*
*who've given me more than I expected,*
*and far more than I deserve.*

## Stephen

Myra came into my life exactly when I needed her. She worked with my younger sister. We met when I was twenty-six and she was twenty-three. I was home between tours, and she liked my army greens. She didn't particularly like me, she confessed that later, but she did like my uniform. I was an enlisted man, a sergeant, and although we were permitted to wear civilian clothes when we were returning home, I did not. I wore my rumpled greens with pride. Some flaunted it and would fight at the first chance they got, but I handled it differently. Usually we'd fly into McChord Air Force Base, but from time to time we'd fly commercial and land at Seattle airport. Those were the times when we sometimes ran into problems. Most civilians were good to us. In fact some of them thanked us and told us how proud they were that we were being of service. There were always some people who needed to take a shot though, and from time to time I seemed to attract them.

I had a system. If I ran into trouble I'd walk around the troublemakers and try to kill them with kindness. I saw too much pain and hurt during my two tours in Afghanistan; I didn't need that when I got home. The first couple of times, the other men in my platoon would try to pull me into it. I was one of the bigger men, but that wasn't for me. If there was a problem and somebody needed to be helped out I'd step in, but to be tough just for toughness' sake, that's not what I'm about. It never has been. So, if we were at the airport and somebody walked into my path or made a smart remark, I'd excuse myself and tell them to have a nice day. It always surprised them. After a while one or two of the other men started doing the same thing. It was better than getting angry. There's no point in that.

The first time I met Myra I'd done my trick at the airport and I felt good. Two college-age, football-player types had walked into my path, and I stepped around them. *Yes, I'll keep you safe so you can chase the sorority girls around, no worries, guys.* Like I said, I'd seen enough; I didn't need to deal with it when I got home. I'd walked around the two heroes, and I was letting them have their giggles and make their smart remarks when an older voice hissed.

"Shame. Shame on you."

When I turned around I could see an elderly lady reprimanding the two boys. She stood her ground, and the two of them shuffled off, embarrassed but trying not to show it. I smiled at her and waved as I rushed toward the big, sliding glass doors, trying to catch my bus. I thought about that lady all the way home and wondered whether she might have lost someone in her own war, or whether she just had a little more feeling for her country than the boys did. It didn't matter. I should have gone back and thanked her and walked her to wherever she was going. I was still thinking about her when I saw Myra sitting on the couch in my younger sister's living room.

I knocked on the front door and walked in, the way I always did. Allyson would be doing what she was always doing—running around the house chasing after my niece or nephew. Myra didn't look at me. She looked at my uniform—my shirt, my pants—and then down to my shoes.

"Your shirt needs to be ironed. You look like you've been living rough."

That's when she finally met my eyes.

"Well, the hotels have been four stars instead of five so yeah, it's been a bit rough. Where's Ally?"

She heard my voice, and the tornado that's my little sister came running toward me. Her five feet one and a half inches couldn't knock me over, of course, but she always gave it a good shot. It had been twelve months, and nothing felt better than having Allyson holding on to me and gripping me close.

"I would have come. We would have come. Mike's been waiting for you to call. You need to call, Stephen, you don't need to take a cab."

"I took the bus, it's good. It's all good."

And it was. The dark-haired, mysterious girl on the couch kept watching me, and I was home for six months in the safest place in the world. No gunshots, no explosions, nobody trying to kill me and my men. Just home.

I found out that Myra and Allyson weren't really friends; they were just coworkers. Myra was getting over a relationship where she'd been hurt, and when Allyson said "hurt" she lingered on the word, giving the impression that the hurt was perhaps more than just emotional. I was training in Fort Lewis, a fifteen-mile commute from Allyson and Mike's home in Olympia, just south of Seattle. Afghanistan still loomed; I knew I was going back. I was infantry and the army needed my platoon for another tour, but for six months I was assigned to teach new recruits about the gong show they were flying into. I was glad to help. They'd give me a little operational training, a bit of a break, and then back to the country where death hung in the air. You don't get used to it. You become friends with men and then you lose them. I never learned how to accept it, but I did learn how to deal. I had a system. I'd hold on to the little bit of hope that I had in my heart and do the best I could to keep my own ass safe and help look after the men around me. The hope I had, the hope I held on to, was the family I didn't have. My sister and her husband, Mike, had created what I wanted, and I was happy for them. My nephew was three and my niece was two. Allyson and Mike worked hard, and although they didn't have much they were doing it together, as a family. I kept my hopes alive inside me, knowing it was possible, and believing that one day it would be my turn.

Most days, I left the base mid-afternoon after an early morning start, and I'd head to Allyson's workplace. Myra and she worked in one of those huge mega-supermarkets. It was part of a mall that always seemed like it was being expanded. As two of the gazillion cashiers who worked there, their breaks were at the same time every day. At first I'd make sure I was there by three in the afternoon so I could have a few minutes with my sister that weren't interrupted with her cooking dinner or looking after the kids. Then, when I found out Myra's break was fifteen minutes before Allyson's, I started arriving even earlier, accidentally on purpose.

She had a strange way about her that lured me in. I hadn't been in many relationships, and maybe I was too trusting. I'd been overseas trying to protect a way of life that was being threatened, but maybe that way of life had become too idyllic in my mind. Maybe I confused what life was supposed to be like with what it actually was like. I knew I wanted what my sister and her husband had. I wanted it badly, and I made my own decisions. No one lied to me or tricked me, and Myra was a very beautiful girl.

She'd push me away and pull me toward her at the same time. When I arrived she'd be sitting by herself outside the lunchroom door at the back of the store, reading a magazine or talking to the construction workers from the building next door. No matter what the weather, she'd have the top couple of buttons on her cashier uniform unbuttoned, and she'd usually lean forward when she spoke, teasing whoever dared to look.

"You're missing your sister, soldier boy. Or is there something else bringing you here?"

My tough, Afghanistan-toured face reddened a little as the construction guys went back to their work, laughing to each other. I sputtered out an answer.

"I like the dust from the building. It reminds me of where I came from."

Then, as though she was feeling bad about mocking me, she patted the ground beside her, inviting me to sit. She would lean so close that I could smell the sweet fragrance of her hair. It was like wild flowers and strawberries. And, when she looked at me with her flirtatious, not-so-innocent eyes, I forgot all about where I'd been. I listened to her stories about her coworkers, her managers, the movie stars in her magazine, and I didn't hear a word. All I saw was a beautiful dark-haired girl who smelled like wild flowers and strawberries.

I tried putting my arm around her once. I stroked her back, and then placed my big, clumsy hand on her shoulder and ran it down her side. She tensed up. The girl who would bump into me, and briefly nestle her head under my chin, tensed up and moved away. She was so hard to understand. On the few occasions, which she initiated of course, when she would touch my face or my hand, I could feel her softness. It was her softness that I wanted. I wanted to place my hands on the narrow curves of her waist, pull her close to me, and feel that softness. She drove me crazy, and as the days went by I couldn't stop thinking about her.

I'd hang around once the girls went back to work, after their breaks. I'd walk the streets, or watch the progress of the guys building on to the mall, and then I'd ride home on the bus with Allyson. Their home was mine when I wasn't overseas, and it worked out well for all of us. The six months I was there changed their lives. I was able to spend time with my niece and nephew in the evenings, and it freed up Allyson and Mike to occasionally have some time away for themselves. I hardly took up any room at all. My bedroom was like a large walk-in closet. It had room enough for a single bed against the wall, and I had my duffel bag buried underneath it. It was all I needed, and the familiar sounds of their home showed me what normal was like, as I tried to forget what I'd been through overseas.

My daily trips to the supermarket became a habit, and we were riding home on the bus when Allyson tried to give me advice on the girl I couldn't stop thinking about.

"Maybe you should invite her to dinner, or to a movie. I'd tell you to bring her to the house but you wouldn't have any privacy. Maybe it's time for you to have some fun, Stephen. Just be careful."

I've never known what that meant. Did "being careful" mean taking precautions? And were the precautions of the physical intimacy or emotional intimacy type. I loved my sister and although I was two years older, she always seemed to be the smarter one, the one who knew best. We were barely out of high school when our folks were killed in a car accident. Some things aren't fair and that was one of them. Tragic as it was it brought us closer together. We looked after each other, and I didn't sign up until she was married. By that time she was with Mike, and he was a good man. I liked him, and I knew they were going to be okay. As close as we were though, there were still some things I wasn't going to discuss in depth with her. She was still my little sister, plus she worked with the girl I was interested in, so I kept my answer simple.

"I'll be careful."

It was a short bus ride home, and we were sharing a bench seat. I was on the outside, hanging over the edge, trying to give her as much room as I could. I could feel her smiling her *little sister who thinks she's my big sister* smile. I didn't have to look around to see it. I knew it was there. I'd seen it before.

"She's been through a lot, and I know you have too. I know that, Stephen."

She paused as though she was rethinking her position, considering.

"You should be allowed to have some fun though. Yes, you should. If you're going to do it then you should do it, just, well, be careful."

While I was sitting beside her, she'd had a whole discussion in her head about the merits of whether I should pursue Myra, and she'd decided it would be okay. I put my arm around her, and there was no hesitation. She snuggled close to me, and we stayed in that position all the way home.

There are things you crave when you're not home, in America. Some men miss their mother's or their wife's cooking. Others miss being close to the action, whether it's their favorite sports team or a family event, and everybody misses physical intimacy. If there's one thing that's talked about more than anything else while you're away, it's sex. If you taped the conversations that infantrymen have while they're serving, most would begin with "When I get home I'm going to…" And most of those same conversations would end with the soldier talking about what he was going to do with his wife or girlfriend, the moment he got home. And those who didn't have a partner waiting for them were going to find a woman, at any cost, immediately when they returned to the States and show her what twelve months of loneliness does to a man. I'd never had anybody waiting for me. I'd met a nice girl after my first tour, and we spent some time together while I was home, but when she realized that I really was going back overseas, she found a reason to break off the relationship. We managed to have some intimacy before the break up and that was nice, but that wasn't what I was interested in. I wanted what my sister and her husband had.

I was human, and I still had urges, but sex wasn't at the top of my list. That changed when I saw the dark-haired girl, with her long legs tucked under her, sitting on my sister's couch. Myra looked like sex. Yes, it is possible. When she looked at me, her mouth would part and she had this crooked little smile. It was as though she were saying, "Go on; ask me. I might just say yes."

I'd never met anyone like her before. She had shiny eyes and tanned skin, and even on a rainy western Washington day she had this intense energy that would warm me up. And I wanted physical intimacy with her. I wanted it more than I'd ever wanted it with anyone.

Our first date was a trip to the local fair. I threw darts at balloons that were taped to a wall and won her a small stuffed toy. When the man behind the counter gave it to her, she grabbed it and threw her arms around me. The closeness almost drove me over the edge. I wanted to pick her up and pull her behind one of the stalls and kiss her, hold her. As the evening wore on, it didn't stop; it kept building. By the time we'd ridden on our fourth amusement ride, our legs jostling against each other and her long, lean body rubbing against me while the ride shuttled back and forth, I could hardly stand it. She must have felt it too, and when we hit the ground she pushed me toward a concession stand. Smiling, she took me around the side of it, away from the folks lining up for their cotton candy and hot dogs.

"Okay, soldier boy, let's get it over with."

She held her face in front of mine, inches away, her lips, waiting, ready. The top buttons on her blouse were undone, showing the lovely, long lines of her neck. It took every bit of me to keep focusing on her eyes. I knew what she wanted. I just wasn't sure what I'd done to merit it.

"I don't understand."

"I can't get rid of that bulge in your pants."

I stepped back a little, embarrassed, and her smile became kinder, softer.

"It's okay. It's a compliment. I understand. I just can't do anything about that tonight. It's too soon, but you should kiss me. We should kiss and see what it feels like. And then it's done. We'll have done it."

I needed no further encouragement. I leaned forward and after a soft brush of our lips, I eagerly put my mouth on hers and kissed her for the first time.

We stayed that way with our faces close for a moment. I think I may have been holding my breath, because I could feel her hot breaths hitting my face. Then, she looked down at my still-present erection.

"Didn't work. It's still there. The kiss was good though."

She stayed close, staring into my eyes.

"The kiss was nice, Myra. That was really nice."

And it was. It was a special kiss. It felt as though we were meant to be kissing and that our lips had been designed with each other in mind. As far as I was concerned, they fit together perfectly.

"Yes, Stephen, it was a nice kiss."

She moved away from me after that, but she reached back and held on to my hand and kept holding it for the rest of the night.

Sometimes we'd stay in and look after my niece and nephew. We'd watch television with the volume turned low after they'd gone to bed, always with an eye on the living room door, in case they got restless and decided to investigate what their uncle was up to. Other times we'd take walks through the streets of Olympia, talking about all the changes that were happening and what we thought things would be like in the months or years ahead. I told her how much I wanted stability, a family, and she told me she wanted the same. She'd been through something, I didn't know what, but it was time for her to settle down too.

All the while it was as though a huge clock hung over our heads. The clock kept ticking, and the hands moved around so fast. At first I had months before I was due to be deployed again, and then it was less than two months. All of a sudden, I was in my final week. It happened too quickly.

We spent my last evening together. At first we didn't talk about it as though it was going to be our final night, but we knew it would be.

She lived in the basement of her parents' home, a crowded little space, jammed with boxes and mementoes of the family members who didn't live there anymore. Her brother was in Canada, and she didn't say much about her sister other than that she'd moved away. Myra had lived with a boyfriend until a short time before we met, and when the relationship ended she moved in with her parents out of necessity. Each time I visited more boxes infringed on the small living area that she had to herself. We joked that perhaps the boxes were her parent's way of hinting that soon there would be no room left for her in their home.

Sometimes she cooked upstairs in their kitchen, but that night we ordered a pizza and when we finished she didn't turn on the television. Instead she took my hand and led me to the small bedroom adjacent to her living room. It wasn't the first time. We'd shared each other's bodies a few weeks into our relationship. We'd discovered that much the same way our lips seemed to join together perfectly, our bodies did too. She had an insatiable desire, and although I'd never found myself to be an Olympic champion with anyone else, with her I was able to make love several times in an evening. This night was different though. It was our last night and after we made love, it felt like we'd sexed the urges right out of each other. That night we were looking for something else.

We lay side by side on her narrow bed, watching each other. There were windows, high on the walls looking out to ground level from her little basement space, and the cold December wind rattled against them.

Even though I saw lots of pain and suffering when I was away, I never talked about fatality, because I never believed anything bad was going to happen to me. I believed there was a plan, and that plan involved my having a family, just like my sister had. When our parents died, Allyson and I each had our bad days. Fortunately, there weren't too many of them that happened at the same time. One of us was always there to help the other. There was one day though, several months after they passed, when we were missing our folks so much, and we both felt like giving up. The minister, the one who'd performed the service for our parents, came by to check on us, and he seemed to recognize that we were struggling. He was a good man. I don't know if he had to follow up. Maybe it was part of his job, or maybe it wasn't. For some reason he decided to come see us that day, and I'll never forget what he said: "God didn't bring you this far to drop you now."

That was all, but it was all we needed to hear. Whenever I've been overseas, I've always thought there was something good coming for me, something better, and that somebody was looking after me. I wanted to tell Myra, to reassure her that I'd be back, but it wasn't that easy. You have to feel it; you have to believe it yourself. So, when she started to speak, I touched her lips with my finger and shook my head, imploring her not to finish.

"You might not come back…"

She pushed my finger away. "It's true, Stephen, I might not see you again. Then what happens? All this was for nothing?"

I hadn't seen her cry. It had been six months of happy, sexy, funny days and nights. When I'd tried to ask her about her boyfriend, the one who broke her heart, she wouldn't talk about him. She told me there was no reason to experience the sadness all over again. This was different though. I knew she'd never let me see her cry. She wouldn't allow that. Instead her expression became intense, almost angry.

"I'll be back. It's twelve months. I'll be back by Christmas time next year."

I lost her. For a long moment I lost her. Her eyes were still on me, but I knew she was thinking of something else, or maybe someone else. So, I made a decision. We wanted the same things. I knew we did. We'd talked about them as we walked around the city, looking at the houses with families safely living their lives inside them. She wanted stability, and children, just like me. So, I asked her, and she didn't even think about it. She just said yes.

The next day we hurriedly purchased a license and bought each other simple gold bands. Then we found a sympathetic justice of the peace who agreed to waive the usual three-day waiting period. Later that morning, we stood in a county courtroom and carolers sang outside, shaking their collection plates, singing about a Christmas I wasn't going to see. My brother-in-law stood resolutely on one side of me, and my sister reluctantly, after telling me how crazy I was, stood beside Myra, witnessing our short ceremony. And the girl with the dark hair and long legs took my last name and became Myra Brown. It was December fifteenth, ten days before Christmas. That night, my sister and Myra drove me the few miles to McChord Air Force Base, and I hooked up with my platoon. From there I was shipped back to hell, back to Afghanistan for twelve more months, leaving my new wife behind.

## Becky

James and I met while we were in college. He was sharing a small apartment just off campus and I was living with my parents. He'd arrive at my parents' home, usually covered in the Seattle rain, out of breath, running from the bus stop, and he'd always look dashing. Yes—dashing, there was no other way to describe him. He had darting blue eyes and a smile that made you want to smile back, and his fair hair was terminally unkempt. And he had this friendly face that always managed to coax the goodness out of people. James was a very good man, and it shone through him.

When he got to my parents' house he'd be soaking wet and smiling and happy to see me, and he'd touch my hand. That was always the first thing he'd do. I tried to tease him sometimes and throw myself into his arms, but somehow he always found my hand and held it. It was as though he needed to touch it to make sure it was really me.

He'd place my hand in his and let out a sigh.

"Okay, Becky, we're good now. We're good."

Then, we'd do the hug and kiss thing. If my mom or dad were watching, it would be a quick peck and embrace, but if they weren't close we'd tend to lose control and fall into each other's arms. He was always cautious, and never wanted to offend or upset my parents.

I didn't come from a particularly religious family and neither did he. I attended Sunday school a few times as a child, but my parents weren't regular churchgoers, and James came from a family of lapsed Catholics. If the topic of religion ever came up, he always said the same thing.

"I'm Catholic, but don't tell anybody, we're hiding from them."

It was one of his few jokes, and it usually got him some laughs, but once, the other person did take offense.

We were at a party at someone or other's house during the rainy college days, and James gave his practiced line to a woman who had been filling us in on the activities at her local chapel. Her mouth hung open in mock horror when he said it, and she looked at him as though he'd just burped up his appetizers.

"We're really not interested in you. We don't recruit people, or try to get them to come back for that matter."

I'm not sure if either of those things were true or not, but we were kids, nineteen years old, still finding our way.

I hadn't formed steadfast opinions on anything yet, including religion, and I don't think James had either.

"I'm sorry. I didn't mean to offend you. I just meant that I don't attend church any more. I've kind of developed my own way of living."

Buzz! Wrong thing to say.

"Your own religion? Yes, there's lots of that going around these days." She sighed, as though she was taking pity on us, but then she seemed to change her mind and continued. "You're right. There are many different religions, but there is only one God. You do realize that, don't you?"

She raised her voice as she asked her question, obviously inviting us, or anyone else within earshot, to debate her point. James and I weren't like that. He was taking business administration, and I wanted to be an art teacher. We studied for exams, held each other close when we watched movies, and respected our elders. We were good people; we just didn't go to church. When the woman confronted us, I suppose I was kind of stunned and didn't know what to do, but James did. Even at nineteen he knew the power of those blue eyes and that smile. He leaned forward, gave her his practiced look, and told her the last thing she wanted to hear.

"Yes, I'm sure you're right."

Oh my gosh, she was so angry. She wanted to debate her point so badly, but James wouldn't let her. Then, as though it was the most natural thing in the world, he took my hand and looked me in the eyes.

"We have that thing, Becky. We need to go."

It looked like smoke was about to come out of the woman's ears. I don't know if I spoke or just mumbled and nodded, but I got up very quickly and we left. We managed to stifle our laughter until we were all the way outside. He'd borrowed his mother's car for the night, and we made it right up until we were sitting safely in our seats, well out of earshot. As soon as he looked at me, it was over though. I started laughing so hard that I let out a snort.

"I don't think I've ever done that before. I don't think I've ever snorted."

I could barely get the words out between my bouts of laughter.

"It's a cute snort, as far as snorts go. I mean I've heard a few, and I would say yours is the cutest."

I slapped him on the shoulder, and that was when I felt it. In that moment, I felt like I was truly part of a couple. It's hard to explain. I mean, I'd felt as though he was my boyfriend for quite a while, but that night things changed.

With our shared exit and the way he made sure I was okay and held my hand as we left, and of course, my snort, it kind of cemented everything. It made me feel as though it was James and me against the world. It was like all of a sudden feeling this thing and saying to myself, "Okay, this is that feeling. This is how I've wanted to feel for a long time. I just didn't realize this was the way I wanted to feel."

I liked it. I liked the feeling and wanted more, and when my laughter subsided, I told him, in the way that girls tell boys these things.

"I love you."

I wanted him to be the first to say it. We'd been dating for four and a half months, and it almost felt like he was going to say it sometimes, but it never quite happened. It didn't matter. I said it because I felt it, not because I thought it was the proper time to say it.

He answered right away, and in typical James fashion, every word sounded as though it was coming from somewhere deep inside him.

"Oh man, I love you too, Becky. I really do."

And that was it. We loved each other and we knew it. At first we said it all the time, and then we only said it when we were close, and of course we said it on our wedding day a whole lot of times. I'm jumping ahead though. There's more, lots more, and I should probably share the intimate details too; it's just that there weren't many. Or, there weren't many before we were married that is. It wasn't that we were prudes, we were just good people and I'd made a decision not to have sex until I was married, and James respected that. Did he want more? Yes, I'm sure he did, but he never pushed. We'd sit on my parents' sofa when they were out for the evening, and he'd slide his arm over my shoulders, and I'd nuzzle close to him. Then he'd kiss my neck and my cheeks, and my forehead. Eventually, when I couldn't take it anymore, I'd put my hands on either side of his soft face and pull his lips onto mine.

Sometimes he'd slide his hands up my sides, from my waist, with his fingers dangerously reaching for my breasts. Then he'd rub through my blouse, waiting for me to sigh in pleasure, and I always did. At first, it was involuntary. His thumbs would hone in on my nipples, through the material, and then, his nice soft hands would cup around my breasts, and I had no choice. I just breathed in and out because it felt so good. I'd lift my whole body up in anticipation and wait for the moment when his hands would touch my breasts.

He was different from other men when it came to my body. I'd always had men stare at my chest. Their eyes would be all over my boobs, and then they'd look up and tell me how pretty my curly blonde hair was, or how beautiful my eyes were. Not James though. Oh, he still looked, but it wasn't the same with him. It was like he was entitled to. He always seemed to love the way he could bring his hands up from my narrow waist, and each time he did, he had the same surprised expression on his face as though he were discovering my breasts for the very first time.

After a while, my sigh was a little forced, I admit that, but I couldn't disappoint him. I loved to see that look of satisfaction on his face each time his hands touched me, and my body sat straight up on the couch. And, besides, that was the only satisfaction he was getting in those days.

For the most part, our naked bodies, I mean our whole naked bodies, were a surprise to each of us on our wedding night, and that's the way I wanted it to be. That's the way it's supposed to be.

He was scholarship boy, armed with scholarships from every organization you've never heard of, and my parents paid for my schooling. James's parents weren't as well off, and they did what they could to help him, but for the most part he improvised. He applied for and received scholarships from the Local Order of everything. He had money coming from the Jaycees, the Lions, the Order of Odd Fellows, and any other organization you can imagine. In fact he wrote letters canvassing organizations that didn't even offer scholarships, and several of them kicked in funds also. They were always so pleased to have someone like James apply. He wasn't just a straight A student; he was more than that. He was a mentor. He helped others all the time. After school, he'd work with other students, boys and girls who needed help on exams and projects, and he made sure he humbly mentioned that in his applications. And he was personable, so when the organizations of retired lion tamers, or whoever he found, asked him to stop by for an interview, he always impressed them.

We had a place that we'd go; I suppose every young couple does. We had areas of the school where we'd meet, and we had my parents' sofa, and his mother's car, but we also had Treshingham. Treshingham is a building on the outskirts of Seattle, in Auburn. At one point Treshingham was a bustling factory employing hundreds of people, or it might have been a building where the CIA interrogated international spies, or it might have been a school. We didn't know. It was an abandoned building, and it had its name stamped on an ominous-looking old sign forged onto one of its side walls. Other than that, there were no clues telling us what its purpose had once been. The windows were mostly smashed or missing altogether and it had a dull, grey pallor to its brickwork, but there was something about it. There was something majestic about Treshingham.

We found it when I needed to take a photo of a building for a school project. I needed to tell a story from a picture, and the picture needed to tell a story. My classmates took pictures of things like restaurants or bakeries; one boy even took a picture of a massage parlor. They were all too obvious. The purpose of the exercise was to have the building subtly tell its own story. The person viewing the picture should conjure up a story in their head from the image itself. That's what Treshingham did to us, every time.

We were driving around looking for inspiration, trying to find a building for my project, and it stood out like, well, like Treshingham. It was in the middle of a large empty lot, and it seemed like it had been forgotten. There were homes around the lot, but even they were facing the other way, as though they didn't want to look at the old building, whatever it once was. We could have found out what it once housed quite easily I suppose. We could have researched it, or we might even have chanced upon some elderly person walking in the neighborhood and asked them, but we didn't want to know. We preferred to draw our own conclusions. At first we visited it a couple of times to take pictures of the archways at the back, or through the windows into its long ominous hallways, but then we'd visit just to see if it was still there. I'd pack us a picnic, and we'd sit under the shelter of its overhangs or in the area around it, and each time we arrived, we'd tell a different story about its origin.

James was the most creative. Business administration was wasted on him. He should have been involved in something that utilized his imagination much more effectively.

"I read about it," he lied. "I found an old newspaper article that laid it all out, fascinating story, absolutely fascinating."

He wouldn't look at me while he spun his tales. He stared off into the distance as he pulled a sandwich from the backpack and straightened the blanket before sitting down.

"Tell me, honey, tell me what you've found." Then, I paused, and cut him off just before he launched into his tale. "Tell me what you've found, this time."

He could always make me laugh. Always.

"Testing, Becky, testing. Treshingham was a top-secret facility owned by the United States government. It was used as a joint venture between our government and our spy cousins overseas in British intelligence. This is where they tested all the gadgets that spies used all over the world."

"That's fascinating, honey. Why'd they close it down?"

He gave me a knowing look, the way experienced spies do.

"Somebody talked, Becky, same old story, somebody talked. For years no one knew what happened here, none of these houses were here at the time of course, and Treshingham, or T Building as it was referred to, was the best kept secret in the country. Then, one of the Brits, over here to exchange information, got a little too tipsy one night at a local bar and let the secret out to a waitress. It's sad, but because of his indiscretion, they had to close the whole place down."

My boyfriend, the spy expert, stared up at the old building as though he was remembering happier days when they tested out whatever it was that spies needed to test out.

"What was her name, honey?"

"I'm sorry, Becks? Whose name?"

"The waitress, James, what was the waitresses's name?"

He looked over at me and gave me his blue-eyed smile.

"Ah, I should have known. You always need the name, don't you, Becky?"

I smiled my own cutest, practiced smile back at him.

"It was Trixie, honey. The waitresses's name is always Trixie. She still lives around here somewhere apparently, in one of these houses."

And so the stories went, each time more fantastic and fabulous than the time before. He became an accomplished fabricator of untruths, and after a while, I gave up and didn't contribute my own versions of the old building's history. I couldn't compete, and I was much happier listening to his.

It's where he proposed of course. There was no other place; it had to be there.

It was December, and although our area, in the western part of Washington State, doesn't always get snow, it was unusually cold that day. It felt like the white stuff was probably going to pay us a visit. We drove out of the city, past the department stores that had nativity scenes in their front windows, and the small corner stands with their Christmas trees all lined up and tied together, waiting to be sold. There was a heavy frost on the ground and the wind was whipping it up, making it seem as though a light snowfall whirled around us. I hadn't wanted to go, but he insisted. He told me he wanted to go one more time before the end of the year, so I layered myself with my heaviest blouse, my wool sweater, and the winter parka that my dad had bought me the Christmas before. We sat in the car and ate the lunch I'd packed. The frost flurried around and settled on the little tufts of grass that stuck through the cracks in the blacktop. It looked nice, but it still didn't make sense. It was two weeks before Christmas. We should have been wrapping gifts or deciding how we were going to spend our time over the holidays, not sitting at Treshingham.

He'd been fidgety, and that should have been my first clue, but I didn't know. I really didn't. We'd eaten a little, and I just wanted to hold my boyfriend's hand, turn the heater up high, and drive home. He had other ideas though.

"I found something."

He wasn't staring off in the distance as he said it; he was looking at me with a very non-James serious-type expression on his face.

I thought something was wrong. I thought he was going to tell me he'd found a lump on his head or perhaps in an even more sensitive area. I slid along the bench seat of the car, closer toward him, and put my hands on my knees, bracing for the worst.

"You found what, honey? What is it?"

"I need to show you, Becky. Come with me."

He opened his car door and was around at my side, opening mine almost instantly. I let out a little laugh, thinking he was going to tell me another fantastic story, only this time with visual accompaniment. I let him take my hand, just like he always did, and he led me over to one of the rusted old metal doors at the back of our Treshingham.

When we got there, he let go of my hand and took a step away from me.

"Watch this, Becks."

My James kicked the door of the old building and it flew open.

I stood back. I'm not sure why. It was just a deserted building, but I knew we'd tried the doors at one point and they'd seemingly been sealed shut, and he'd managed to open it with just one kick.

Once I was over my initial shock, I peered forward and looked into the dusty hallway.

"Why'd you do that? How did you know that door would open?"

"I came here earlier; I wanted to check something out. Look, Becky, look over there."

I wasn't looking anywhere. He came here without me? No, that didn't compute; I didn't want him coming to our place alone, especially to check something out.

"What do you mean, you came here earlier to check something out. What does that mean exactly, James?"

Yes, my hands were on my hips as I said it, and I was looking at him instead of looking at the sign that was hanging on a door a few feet down the hallway.

He pointed into the dark corridor.

"Honey, look, please look at what I found."

I poked my head into the hall. There was a handwritten note tacked onto a door. I looked over at him and his good, lovely face was smiling at me, telling me that it was going to be okay. I stepped into the hallway and read the note. Then I began to cry.

The note said, "Treshingham Love Factory, Where it All Began."

I'm certainly not a detective, but the note was on a crisp white piece of paper, and there was an inch of dust all around it. I knew who'd hung that note there.

I turned to him and his lower lip quivered. Gently, he pushed me forward.

"Go on, honey, open the door. Open it up."

I took the four or five paces down the hall, pulled the sleeve of my parka over my hand, and turned the dirty old doorknob. It swung open as easily as the main door had, and inside the room there was a table, teetering on three legs, and it had an envelope on it. James was right behind me, but he didn't need to tell me this time. Dirt and dust kicked up as I walked over to the table and picked up the envelope. On the front it said, "For Becky."

I knew that there was more than just a note inside, and I thought I knew what the envelope was going to contain. That's probably why I waited. I didn't wait long, only a few seconds, but I did wait. We'd talked around it and talked about it but never really talked about it for us. I wanted it though, and in that moment I knew for sure that he did too. I just wanted to take a few seconds to have it feel the way it always felt, because I knew that things were about to change.

Inside the envelope there was a folded up piece of paper and, again, in James's handwriting it said, "Becky, will you marry me?" And there was a ring with one shiny little diamond on it. I read the note and held the envelope open, looking at the most beautiful ring I'd ever seen. I almost knocked James over as I turned around and ran straight into him.

I thought it was just me crying, and I was crying, but it wasn't only me. James was crying too, crying and trying to speak at the same time.

"Is that a yes, Becks? Does that mean we're doing it?"

It would have been yes no matter how he'd asked me, but this was better. This was something we'd always have, and it was something I'd never forget.

I punched him in the side with one hand while the other held on to him as tight as I'd ever held anyone.

"Of course it's a yes, mister. Of course it's yes."

And that was it. We drove home, and in between making plans for our future I cried my eyes out. I suppose I was crying partially because I felt bad for being angry with him when he kicked the door open and partially because it was just like the first time I told him I loved him. I had this feeling that I loved, and needed, I just hadn't ever known how much I needed it.

"This is going to be a great Christmas, James."

"We're going to have lots of them, Becks. Lots of them."

Somehow, the ring fit perfectly, and I rubbed his arm as he held onto the steering wheel driving us home.

"It's my size, James. You got lucky. You guessed the right size."

"No luck at all, Becky, it's the magic of Treshingham. Luck's got nothing to do with it."

We married six months later, right after graduation. We were very happy and about to become even happier.

## Stephen

It would be my last tour. If I hadn't already made the commitment I wouldn't have gone. Things were different now; I was a married man with a wife waiting for me at home. From the day I left I imagined what it was going to feel like when I returned and how good it would be when I was back with her. We exchanged emails. From time to time I'd be in a secure area, and I'd catch up on her emails and reply to them. Then, we'd be in darkness again, with no contact. Sometimes it would be a week or two, sometimes longer. I'd been through the same routine during other tours. I knew what it felt like to be away, but it was different this time. At first, I thought about my homecoming, and how perfect it was going to feel, but as the days passed the images weren't as vivid. The reunion scene still played out in my head; it just didn't seem as real as it had been when I first left her. All I wanted was for it to happen, and I didn't care how wonderful it was going to be. I just needed to be home, and to see her, to see all of them.

Her emails were positive, optimistic. She told me she'd look for a place for us to live closer to the time I was due to return. That way we could save a little money while she lived at her parents' house, and we could buy most of our furniture together when I got back. She had some things already, and I wrote back that it was time I owned something more substantial than my army duffel bag. She told me in her messages that the boxes in her basement apartment seemed to have stopped multiplying. Even though her parents were anxious for her to move out, they knew that by Christmas she'd be gone, and they seemed to have given her a reprieve. I made my return emails as positive as I could, but there was little I could talk about, so I talked about the future, our future. I didn't want her to know what it was really like. That wouldn't have been fair to her.

Billy Stewart was a Native American Indian with a Scottish last name. He was a corporal who'd recently been assigned to our platoon, and he was older than the rest of us. We were in our twenties and Billy was in his late thirties. That was old for Afghanistan. I didn't know why he was there. I never figured that out until later. Some didn't want to be there, and others thought they were going to be heroes. They all had their reasons. They came for their country or their fathers or to experience what they'd seen in movies or read in books. And sometimes, they came because they had nowhere else to go. I assumed he was one of those unfortunate men. He didn't talk about his history, so I thought everybody must have given up on him. I figured he probably had nothing left so he joined up, and the army sent him to hell along with the rest of us.

We were from the same part of Washington. Both of us knew the Seattle area well, and he lived just outside Olympia, my hometown. I could tell right away that we were going to be friends. I tried not to get close to anybody over there. It was never a good idea. I always tried to keep to myself, but Billy was different. It was hard not to like him. And, the more I liked him, the more I worried. That's the way it goes sometimes.

He was one of the most intelligent people I'd ever met. He'd quote from books I'd never heard of, or he'd talk about his sports teams and tell me who was winning and who was losing. In between his stories, I told him about Myra, the girl I'd married but barely knew, and the life we were going to have when I got home.

"Sounds like you made the right decision, Sarge. It's good to have somebody in your corner. That's important."

There had been no time to take it all in and get used to feeling like I was a married man. It all happened so quickly. Allyson thought it was too soon, but we didn't listen. I wanted it and so did Myra. It made sense. I played with my wedding band, thinking about my wife, thousands of miles away.

"You got anybody waiting, Billy? Is somebody keeping the fires burning for you?"

He laughed and shook his head.

"Nope, the wigwam is currently empty. Maybe someday, but for now there's just me."

We spent our down time talking while the other men played cards or drank beer. Sometimes we'd talk about Olympia or Seattle, or he'd tell me about a book he was reading, and of course I'd talk about Myra, my new wife. He had a quiet way of coming into a room, unnoticed. He'd sit in a corner, listening, watching, and after a while someone would wonder out loud where he was. From nowhere, he'd lean forward and smile, and it was as though the darkness opened up and he was showing himself to us. He didn't do it on purpose; it's just the way he was.

The accident happened during a mission that wasn't really a mission. There were two of us, crouched in a ditch. We had camped less than a mile outside a village, and our job was to observe and report. It was a relatively safe area with no problems. An infantry unit preceded us and made it to the target, a small village in the Helmand Province. Our commanding officer radioed back the "All Clear" and ordered us to stay put. There's lots of waiting and seeing in the army. You don't know why you're doing it; you just do it. This was one of those times. It was night, but we were in a secure area, so we didn't worry. Billy talked to me about the Cleveland Indians, one of his teams. He didn't care whether they were called the Indians, or the White Men, or the Purple People; it didn't matter to him.

"It's just a name. There's no emotion in a name as far as I'm concerned, Sarge. I mean look at our teams. I mean, the Seattle Seahawks? Please, couldn't they have come up with something more original than Seahawks?"

Then we heard it. A noise that maybe wasn't a noise. A rustle that might have been the wind. He was on his feet and up immediately. I pulled him back down and whispered.

"Wait. Count it. Wait."

I gave it a five count, and we waited and listened. I trained my night vision glasses in a semicircle in front of me, to where I thought I heard the noise. There was nothing there. I gave him the nod, telling him I was going. He was the best. He could sneak into the darkness like no one I'd ever seen, but I was the superior, so I made the decision. If we had to take a chance, I was going to be the one taking it.

I needed to get higher. I needed to see, so I slid myself up onto the ground, out of the ditch, leaving Billy behind. I got up on one knee, listening to the darkness. I was just about ready to give up. I looked ahead and peered into the area in front of me where the noise had come from. There was nothing there. I looked everywhere. Everywhere, except behind me.

The rapid-fire noise of an automatic weapon sounded behind us. I spun backward and fired my weapon in the direction of the noise. It was gone. They were gone. I could hear the sounds of someone retreating. The rounds I'd fired hadn't hit a thing.

Quickly. Think. I was good. I hadn't been hit. We'd been lucky. I thought we were okay. We should have been okay. I slid into the ditch, and he had a tight smile on his face. He was holding his side, just below his hip.

I grabbed the aid kit and the radio at the same time.

"I have a man down. We've been hit. Enemy may have withdrawn. I need medic, and backup. ASAP."

There was no one there; I knew that. They'd watched and waited. It was probably only one man. He'd seen me get up. Billy must have been leaning forward, and the shooter hit him.

"I don't feel anything, Sarge. I don't feel pain. I think I'm okay."

I couldn't understand why the leg of his pants was so heavy until I cut the fabric away. It was soaked in blood. I didn't know a man could bleed so quickly.

He looked at his hands, sopped in his own blood, not acknowledging it.

"It's okay. It doesn't matter. There is no pain, Sarge. It's going to be okay."

As he watched me apply a pressure bandage to the bleeding on the side of his leg, he stopped talking. He looked away, nodding, telling himself he was going to be all right.

The medics were good. They choppered us out and got him in front of a doctor within minutes. The bullets had sliced into the nerves at the top of his right leg. He'd been leaning forward, watching my back, and it was easy pickings for the gunman. If he'd been faster, or braver, he would have aimed higher and maybe got both of us. We were lucky. He'd fired off a round and retreated. It was bad, but it could have been worse.

Unfortunately, Billy was wrong about being okay.

The doctors had no choice. They removed his right leg three inches above his knee.

The day after, when they let me visit him in the military hospital, he was sitting up in his bed, staring forward. When I came in he barely acknowledged me. I sat in the chair beside him. I had no words, and I didn't know what to say. When he did speak we weren't sergeant and corporal any longer. We were just two men who'd been shot at as we crouched in a ditch.

"My own fault. Total disregard for the rules. You had it. I should have been watching behind us. Three hundred and sixty degree coverage, basic, basic, Stephen."

"It wasn't your fault. We were too vulnerable, too alone out there. I should have known that. I should have let you go, and watched your back. I screwed up."

He knew I was right. You get too complacent sometimes. Nothing happens for a while, and when it does, it's to someone you don't know. Then you begin to think you're invincible. You never are though. You're never safe.

We sat for a while, not talking.

"I'll still walk. They're fitting me up, getting me a new leg. And, I'm going home, back to the rain." He seemed resigned, stronger for a moment, as he tried to make me feel better.

I didn't know what to say to him. I had six months left. I was going back to where we'd come from. They'd debrief me, make sure my head was okay, and send me back. Standard operating procedure. It was my job. At the end of the day neither of us knew who was going to be better off, him going home or me back to the lines. That was the harsh reality of it.

"You want me to check in on her, and make sure she's okay?"

I did, but I didn't want Myra to see him the way he was. I didn't want her to worry about me, while I was still back here in the world he was leaving behind.

"That'd be good. I'll get her address to you. That'd be good, Billy."

When I got up, I think both of us knew I'd never get that address to him. He looked at me and nodded, probably accepting that it wouldn't happen, and helping me with my lie.

"I'll see you back home, Stephen. Six months, it'll go fast. Just before Christmas."

He held out his hand and it looked weaker, more fragile than it had out in the field. I held on to it and then cupped my other hand around his.

"You look after yourself. I'll see you in six months."

I'd failed him. My job was to look after my men, and somewhere out there in that ditch I hadn't done my job. I couldn't look back. I closed the door behind me and went back to feed the monster, to give whatever I had left to the army, and to try to keep a little bit of that from Afghanistan.

Becky

My father's name is George, and my mother's name is
Madge, which is not short for Margaret or Marjorie—it's
just Madge. Her parents, my grandparents, in their infinite
wisdom thought that Madge sounded regal, and being
lovers of all things royal, they named my mother Madge.
Thankfully, I was named after neither of my parents, and a
Georgina, or even worse, a little Madge, never happened.
My father teased me from time to time, and told me it was
close, and that I almost became a Georgie or Madgie, but at
the last minute they changed their minds. My mother, who I
suppose at some point resigned herself to the fact that she
was a Madge, would giggle at him and shake her head
when my dad made up his stories. They wanted a boy, and
they got me, and only me. So, when they got to know
James, and especially after we married, George and Madge
got their son, and he was perfect.

And really, he was. James went to work for a waste
management company immediately after college, and
within weeks he was assisting the manager of his
department. Three months later he was receiving job

opportunities from other companies, even some in other industries. That's how he got into the food business. He went from garbage to food within his first working year. We couldn't have been happier, all of us. I made dinner in our little apartment, and we combined celebrating our six-month wedding anniversary along with James's new career move, while my parents sat proudly across the table from us.

"You'll be dealing with food stores then, son, retail mostly, I take it?"

My father was a workingman but also a businessman. He'd managed a building supply store all his adult life. He knew what it was like to get your hands dirty moving concrete blocks around, and he also knew that he needed to sell enough of those concrete blocks each month in order to keep the doors of the building supply store open.

James put his cutlery down and leaned across the table a little, speaking to both George and Madge, when he answered my father.

"Some, George, but restaurants too, a little of both. At first it'll involve a little more knocking on doors and selling than I'd like, but that'll only be temporary until I expand the client list. I'll be establishing their wholesale division all over Seattle and Tacoma, and I can make it whatever it's going to be. The owner of the company tells me that it's mine to build. They've done very little business out this way and they want to change that, so I'm their guy."

My parents beamed at him as my husband focused on his dinner and resumed eating.

"James," I purred, "I thought you were my guy? Wasn't that the deal we made when we got married, honey?"

That's all it took for me to get what I wanted from him. He looked over and gave me his trillion-dollar smile and flashed those incredible blue eyes at me, and only me.

"I'll always be your guy, Becks. They only get to borrow me for a few hours each day."

If the schmaltzy greeting card company had been passing by, they would have taken photographs and written their slogans right outside our window. It couldn't have been much better. Almost everything was falling into place. I say almost because things weren't going so well for me with my career. I made an important discovery when I received my degree in art history. No matter how excellent your grades are, when you present your diploma in art history to the world, you are qualified for very few jobs. After a few weeks of having that drummed into my head, as I scoured the newspapers searching for a position that would suit my lofty ideals, I took a job at the local art museum. Each day, I sat behind a wicket and took the patrons' four dollars and fifty cents when they came in and tried to figure out what our sculptures and paintings were supposed to represent.

From time to time, I'd escort tour groups to their tour guide, and occasionally I'd monitor different displays, but in terms of utilizing the knowledge I'd acquired in four years of college, I may as well have studied how to give change from a twenty-dollar bill. So, it was no great loss when I told everyone my news at dinner. It would be easy to stay home for a year or two, and my career as a money taker at the art museum certainly wouldn't suffer.

"It died," I announced as seriously as I could manage.

This time they all dropped their knives and forks and looked at me. James even turned his chair slightly toward me, even though we were sitting side by side.

"Who died, honey? What is it?"

I knew how my mother had told my father. She'd taken a line from one of the old-time movies they watched. So, that's how I told my parents and my husband, and that's how my mother knew. She let out a gasp, and then covered her mouth and had a secret little smile on her face. Neither of the men clued in. My mom guessed though, and she knew what was coming next—I know she did.

"The rabbit died."

Then, my father knew too. He remembered. I could tell, and he smiled, his big, broad smile. My husband was the only one who wasn't there yet. I suppose he'd probably never heard the expression before.

"We don't have a rabbit, Becky."

When he looked across the table at my parents, they were leaning back in their chairs and they had a "we're going to be grandparents" look on them. And, when he looked at me, I put my hands on my stomach, and I had a "we're going to be parents" look on me. My honor roll, business executive, food services sales manager finally got it, and he flew up from his seat and put his arms around me. Then, just as quickly, he pulled away as though I were fragile.

"Oh, I'm sorry, honey. I mean, I'm happy, but I'm sorry too. I'll be careful, very careful."

It was one of the only times I'd ever seen him look as though he were lost. For a moment, he didn't know what to do, and then he had another realization.

"Christmas, will our baby will be here for Christmas, Becky?"

I nodded at him. "Possibly, James, possibly."

My parents laughed and held each other, and again, the schmaltzy greeting card people were missing out on another beautiful moment. It was good. This was what happy felt like.

Later that evening, after an endless amount of secret smiles from my mother, and my father planning his unborn grandchild's whole future, James and I sat up in bed, and he did the math.

"It must have been during our honeymoon. I know, the dates don't add up, but that's when it was strongest, that's when I feel my sperm was particularly strong."

He was warped, seriously warped. He was warped from smiling too much and warped from trying to change the laws of nature to fit his theory.

"Uh, honey, actually it's pretty simple. I'm two months along, so it happened just about two months ago. So, it was probably during one of your frisky Friday night sessions. Remember, you were so excited about all the job offers that were coming in and couldn't wait to bed me to show me how powerful you were."

He wasn't buying into it. He was at Treshingham all over again, making up stories. He stared straight ahead, changing the laws of nature as he went along.

"Not quite, Becky. I mean, that's kind of how it works but not exactly."

I leaned into his shoulder, snorted a little laugh, and told him to continue.

"Well, as I said, it's simple. There is an initial period of conception, and if the seed is strong enough it will wait for backup."

"No, James, don't do it. Wait for backup? Wait months before more sperm comes and then decide it's going to be a baby?"

He was on a roll. His beautiful, blue eyes looked down at me, reassuringly, twisting Mother Nature to fit his version of events.

"Kind of. Conception that results in, well, a baby, is actually a multiple copulating process."

With those words, I was over the edge. He went on to explain to me that to create a baby you needed to have several marathon lovemaking sessions, and when enough sessions had accumulated, the woman would be with child. I let him have his theory. He was a romantic, and he loved the memory of our honeymoon, and I did too. If James wanted to believe that our baby-to-be began when we first had sex, I wasn't going to argue with him. I was going to be a mother and James was going to be as good a father as my dad was. The feeling that I hadn't recognized at first, the feeling that I'd felt with him in the car on the night we left the party, and later, sitting outside Treshingham, had become a constant part of my life. It was a feeling I hadn't known I needed, and now I had it. It was what I always wanted.

# Stephen

Afghanistan took two more men from us. We lost them
during operations I wasn't part of. Neither was assigned to
my squad, and I didn't know them well, but it still meant
two more brothers or husbands weren't going to make it
home. Fortunately, the other casualties we had in my final
few months were minor. There were no more Billy Stewart
situations, no more blood on my hands. I got lucky; my
enemies became tedium and boredom. That was enough.
They were relentless, and they sapped the energy from me,
but they were manageable. And, there was the dirt and the
dust. The dirt felt like it flowed through my body, and the
dust was on everything, everywhere. I was lucky though, I
made it. Afghanistan let go of me, and on December
fourteenth, after the longest twelve months of my life, the
army sent me home.

I didn't feel the relief until I was on the ground and
walking through the gate. I kept thinking that something
might happen to send me back. As I slept on the plane, I
imagined that I was going to wake up and be back there,
crouched in a ditch watching the blood gush from my

friend's leg, or sitting in a hut, listening for gunfire, waiting to be pulled back into it. So, when I saw them at the airport, all of them, the only thing that mattered was that I wasn't there, and that I didn't have to go back.

"Welcome Home Uncle Stephen" was the first thing I saw when I walked through the gate. My niece and nephew held a homemade cardboard sign aloft, their little arms reaching as high as they could manage. Then I saw her. Mike and Allyson were in front of her, helping the children balance the sign between them. Her tall body bobbed back and forth behind them. I could see her trying to look over the sign, searching for me as her eyes nervously panned the other travelers.

I smelled her scent before she reached me, and she smelled the same. She was still wild flowers and strawberries, and when I reached for her she held on and wouldn't let go. Even as Allyson and my brother-in-law, hugged me, she kept holding on to my side, claiming possession. And she stayed that way, hanging from me, until we made it out of the airport all the way to Mike and Allyson's car.

She'd found us a rental house a few streets away from my sister and a short bus ride to her supermarket. From the outside, it looked like one of the oldest houses I'd ever seen, but it didn't matter. It was ours. I stood outside on the sidewalk, in the middle of them all. Myra was on one side, beckoning me toward the front door, and Mike was on the other trying to shepherd the children and my sister back to their car.

When I managed to pull myself away from Allyson, she walked backward, holding my niece in her arms. She'd turned three while I was away. The baby, crawling on the floor before I left, wasn't a baby any more. When she spoke, she had a little-girl voice, and I could feel every word.

"Never, ever, Uncle Stephen. Never, ever. You promised."

"Never, ever, honey. I promise."

I answered my niece but kept looking at my sister.

Allyson's eyes never left me. She just kept walking backward toward the car, holding her daughter.

"Listen to your niece, Stephen. Listen to her."

"I am. I'm home. I've told them, I'm staying home."

Allyson and I had been through so much together. I don't think I ever truly realized the toll it took on her when I was overseas. If it meant that she wouldn't have to worry about me anymore, then it was an easy promise to make. Things were different now. I hadn't signed up for another tour. I'd work from base or do whatever they wanted me to do, but I wasn't going back.

After watching their car pull away, I followed my wife into the old house, and suddenly, it was Christmas. A tree stood in the corner of the small living room with ornaments hanging from the branches. There were boxes, wrapped in brightly colored paper, spread around the base, and on the walls of the room she'd hung decorations. There was even a cardboard Santa Claus popping out of a chimney, and a painting of a child looking up at a star in the night sky. And, on the far wall, she'd put the sofa from her basement apartment, with the same comfy-looking shawl draped over the side. She stood back, letting me survey the room.

"Christmas. I forgot. Really, I did. I just wanted to get home. I'm sorry."

It was less than two weeks away. Christmas music had been playing in the airport; the plane had even been decorated, with tinsel hanging on the door to the front cabin. I remembered it. It just hadn't registered. All I could think about was getting home.

"I know you did. It's fine. Take a look around. Tell me what you think."

The inside of the house smelled like old house and Christmas tree. It was musty and had a lived-in odor that smelled like it would never go away, but I didn't care. It was luxury compared to where I'd come from. I put my duffel bag in the corner and walked around the living room. There was a large window on each side of the room, and tiny Christmas figurines sat on the sills. From one of the windows you could look out to the back yard, and there was a big, old tree leaning toward the house, its branches precariously brushing against the gutters. She kept her arms folded in front of her chest, watching me. I walked through the hallway and pushed open a door. I loved it, all of it. The bathroom looked like it had been designed a hundred years ago. In the middle of the tiled floor sat an old-fashioned claw-foot tub, with a showerhead hanging on a chain above it. And a mirror, frosted and faded from years of use, was mounted on a cabinet door.

I could smell her, feel her, behind me.

"Come with me, soldier boy. Allow me to demonstrate."

She'd pulled off her jacket and was wearing a tight, black T-shirt and a short, faded jean skirt. Just like before, she was impossible to resist. She took my hand and showed me around, leading me from room to room, all the while performing her silent presentation. I kept nodding and smiling, enjoying watching her, being close to her. There was a bank of cupboards on the wall of the dining room. She made me stand at the entranceway as she opened and closed door after door, demonstrating how each one worked. With each demonstration, her crooked smile beckoned me closer, but when I'd approach she raised the palm of her hand, holding me back, telling me it wasn't time yet. When we went into the kitchen, she angled her body over the countertop and then bent over and touched a door handle, opening it and closing it again. As she leaned over she pushed her bottom into the air, exhibiting her assets, and looked up at me. I could barely breathe as her fingers stroked the countertop. Her lithe body bent over once again, and her long, dark hair fell in front of her face. After each demonstration, she came closer to me, but when I tried to hold her, or touch her, she still kept me at arm's length. Finally, as though she was tired of her game, she beckoned me back into the living room and led me to the window, showing me the large tree out back with its branches leaning against our house.

"Do you like our house? Because if you don't you can sleep outside under that old tree, just like you're used to. That'd be fine too."

Her smile was deliciously lopsided, and her eyes sparkled as she teased me.

"I like it very much, Mrs. Brown. After a demonstration like that how can I not like it?" I wanted her; I just hadn't known how much. You fight the urges. You learn to ignore them. During all the months away, I never realized how badly I needed her body, her softness. She looked at me and a curious expression passed over her face. First it was want, desire, and then it seemed like she was angry.

"You're not going back, Stephen. This is too hard. You can't do this to me again."

In that moment, I knew she loved me. It was more than just an arrangement we'd made where we told each other we wanted the same things. I loved her, and more importantly, she loved me. I could tell. My weary muscles somehow found the strength to pick her up, and I took her in my arms and cradled her. My legs felt like jelly as I made my way to the only room in the house she hadn't shown me. After managing to arouse me in every other room with her flirtatious demonstrations, it was only fitting that we look in the bedroom last.

I didn't see much of the room that first day and night. I know we had a bed, a new one, and the dark curtains were closed over the windows, blocking out the light, but those are the only details of the room that I recall. I do remember the sheets, though, and how warm and clean they felt. And of course, I remember her skin, the soft skin that I'd tried to block from my dreams for the past twelve months.

We fit together the same way we had before I left. I'd missed it, all of it: her long, smooth legs, and the way she looked up at me, tantalizingly flicking her hair back. When I touched her, or kissed her, I felt like I was breathing again after holding my breath for a long, long time.

Our bodies reacted to each other the way they should—mine touching hers, and hers responding back. When she put her arms around me, on my bare back, I could feel her small wedding band, the one I'd placed on her finger before leaving, touching my skin. It was right, the way it's supposed to be. There were no rules. We were close and pleasuring each other, and that's all that mattered.

I slept between our lovemaking sessions. My flights back from hell had taken their toll on me. From time to time, I'd awaken and although she wasn't always beside me, I'd hear her voice, telling me to go back to sleep. Or I'd wake up and feel her close, and need her sex, and we would, and then I'd drift off again, sleeping the sleep of the saved, secure that my life was about to begin.

## Becky

James changed. He was still my James, the man with the piercing blue eyes and dazzling smile, but it was like he reached a new level. Everything he did became more intense. It wasn't that things went bad right away. They didn't; everything was good. His new job was going well. He enjoyed it, and he was very good at it. He charmed the people who ran restaurants and food places all over Seattle and sold them his line of crackers, soups, or authentic homemade Italian pasta that came out of a cardboard box. He just did it. He set sales targets and then exceeded them. He was putting in lots of time, but he tried to do as much as he could from home too. He sat for hours with his laptop balanced on his knees, or at our dining room table, plotting ways to earn more business, or he'd make his calls from the other room, talking to managers, making deals. And in between it all, he couldn't wait to become a father. When he wasn't talking about sales or business, he was talking about our baby or talking to our baby. He'd lean over me and touch my stomach, while I lay back on the couch.

"When you're ready to come out, I'll be here, waiting. I have so much to show you. You're going to like it here."

He'd nod as though he were hearing an answer, a voice coming from my stomach."You're right, take your time, it's nice in there, I know. All I'm saying is, when you get here, I'll be waiting. That's all."

Then I'd smile and he'd kiss me on the forehead before retiring to the other room to sell whatever the owners of his company wanted him to sell to his clients.

My pregnancy was difficult from the beginning. I met other women as I sat in the doctor's waiting room or when I had tests done at the hospital, and they told me their stories of easy deliveries or cravings they had while they were pregnant. I was sick all the time, and the only thing I craved was for it to be over. The doctor told me that morning sickness was normal during the first three months, except it didn't end. I was sick during my fourth month, and by my fifth I could hardly stand it. I kept waiting for it to go away, but it wouldn't. I'd wake up to pains in my stomach and bouts of nausea. They'd go away for an hour or two in the morning sometimes, but by the afternoon or early evening they returned. My back was sore from leaning over toilets and basins being sick. I hated to eat because I knew that inevitably it would come back up. And if the pain wasn't there, I knew it was close by and would come again.

My mother encouraged me. The doctor told me it would pass, and James was always there. No matter what happened, he always tried to be with me, excited about our baby. The doctor ran more tests. He scheduled an ultrasound, and then another one. He took time away from his other patients to attend my last ultrasound, watching the technician scan the hand-held monitor over my stomach. James sat by my side, holding my hand, smiling that everything was going to be okay.

We looked at the monitor together and then at the doctor, waiting for his reaction. He stood behind the technician, letting her do her job, and he tried to alleviate the pressure.

"Is it ticklish, Rebecca? I always wondered that."

James laughed at the doctor's joke, but I couldn't. I needed to know that my baby was okay and, I wanted him to tell me why I was sick and in pain all the time.

"Don't make me laugh, Doctor. What's going on in there? Can you tell?"

He stepped back after barely examining the screen.

"You're fine, Rebecca. You're fine and the baby seems to be healthy too. You're experiencing some nausea. It'll pass, and then in just over three months you'll have a tenant who'll live with you rent-free for the next eighteen years or so."

I half-expected James to slip the doctor his business card as he gave him his sales-executive laugh and jumped up to shake his hand.

"Thank you, Doctor. Thanks for being here."

It was good enough for James; he heard what he needed to hear. We watched as the doctor opened the door and left us, his long white lab-coat swinging back and forth. It wasn't good enough for me though. I needed to know what was going on inside of me.

"I'm so sick of being sick. I'm sick all the time. This can't be right. Why don't I feel better?"

The technician shrugged, and told me it wouldn't be much longer. James touched my hand, the way he used to, and told me to be strong. I was being strong. It wasn't my fault. None of it was. I knew something was wrong; it had to be.

We moved to a larger apartment. James handled everything. He found us a place a few blocks from my parents' house. It had three bedrooms: enough space for a baby room and an office for him. Then, my father and he became interior decorators. They put up wallpaper in the baby's room. The design had colored letters of the alphabet lined up along the top of the wall by the ceiling. And they assembled our baby's crib and placed it in the middle of the room, where the light from a window settled on it. Then, they arranged all the toys that had begun to accumulate, on the shelves in the room, and inside the crib. Somehow, between all the time James was devoting to dealing with clients and making sales, he managed to move us in and arrange everything, while I did very little. Our parents helped too, but I couldn't. Every time I moved I felt more pain or thought I was going to be sick.

Everything was put into boxes and moved in one weekend. The new place was brighter, and larger, and the baby's room looked beautiful. It couldn't be any better. I just needed our baby to arrive. It was three months away, and I couldn't wait. I just wished it would happen faster.With a month to go we picked names—Margaret if she was a girl and Michael for a boy. My fingers were so swollen that I had to wear my wedding ring on a chain around my neck, and my ankles ballooned up so much that by halfway through the day I could barely walk because it hurt so much. And I was still sick. That part never did go away.

The day that it happened, James wasn't home. It wasn't his fault; he was trying to build his career and make things easier for us. I hadn't been able to work. The days when I was ill had run together so much that I stopped going in. Someone else could make change at the museum for a while. I was sick in the morning as usual, but by ten my stomach was empty and for a short, glorious hour I had no nausea and no pain. I actually felt quite calm. I stood at the sink, in the kitchen of our new apartment, washing carrots and putting them into a bowl of water, readying the night's dinner hours in advance. And then the pain started. It was sharp and in my abdomen, and it was bad. I knew it was bad. I called my mother, and when she arrived she called the ambulance right away.

They all knew; I think my mother even knew. The ambulance attendants quickly examined me. The paramedic was an older woman, and she took charge of the situation right away. She told her partner and me at the same time.

"We're admitting her. Advise Emerg that we're on our way."

With sad, resigned looks on their faces they quickly loaded me onto a stretcher and wheeled me out to their vehicle. They were rushing, but they weren't panicked. Nobody would tell me anything. I just kept holding my stomach, not wanting to look down, thinking about my baby.

When we arrived at the hospital, the nurse told me that everything was going to be okay. My mom wiped my forehead with a cloth. There were tears in her eyes as they wheeled me into an operating room. At one point I asked for James and for my dad. I know I did. I remember that. From the point that door swung behind me with my mother telling me she loved me, I don't remember anything. I can't, and I won't. I choose not to remember anything that happened in that room.

The first thing I saw when I woke up was the garland on the wall. It was hanging down on one side as though someone had begun to decorate for Christmas and then got called away. It took me a few moments to remember where I was. They'd put me into my own room; I could see that. James was beside me, and my dad was close too, leaning against the wall, the worry lines on his face deeper than I'd ever seen them. My mother quietly slipped through the door, with a paper coffee cup in each hand. She looked like she'd been walking fast, and she smiled when she saw that my eyes were open. It didn't feel as though I'd just woken up. It felt as though I'd been there all the time listening to them, and that I'd just decided to join in.

James spoke first, trying to be strong, but something was missing from his face, his eyes.

"Becks, you're awake, we were worried. It's going to be okay."

He wanted to fix it. I could see that already, but there was nothing to fix. Something had left us, something we'd had, and now it was gone.

My mother came close; they all watched me, wanting to know if I knew. It was my mom who tried to tell me.

"Becky, you need to know. The baby…"

"I know, Mom."

I did not cry. I held my head still. I'd think about my baby, the baby they hadn't met, when I was alone. I was entitled to that.

James put his face on my chest and gripped onto my arm, still trying to fix it.

"You're okay, that's all that matters. It's going to be okay, Becky."

They left. My mother and father said more, lots more. They told me they loved me and that we live for a long, long time. I suppose that meant that we'd have other opportunities. They told me how proud they were of me, and then, somewhere between their tears and common sense, they picked up their jackets, left us, and went home.

James wouldn't leave me. The first night he slept on the small bench that was beside my hospital bed. He'd reach over from time to time, stroking my hand or touching my shoulder. I wanted him there; he had to be there, but I needed to be alone too. I needed to say goodbye.

They kept me in the hospital, and at first they wouldn't say for how long. They wanted to observe; that was all they told me. That wasn't enough. I needed more. You get to a point where you need a specific time, and when the nurse told me I was going home the next morning I knew what I needed to do. James had gone for a walk to get some air, and when he stepped through the door, trying to be quiet, I could feel the cold from outside coming from his jacket, his skin. I was sitting up, waiting for him.

"It's warm in here, you're lucky. Feels like winter outside, Becks."

"You need to go home, James. Go home and get everything ready. They're letting me out of here tomorrow. Pick me up in the morning, honey."

He started to tell me that he wasn't leaving, that he was going to spend the night with me again, but I cut him off. He needed to go. It took him a moment before he realized what he had to do, and then he held my face in his hands and kissed my forehead.

"I love you, Becky."

He meant every word, I'm sure he did, and just like he used to, he'd pulled them from somewhere deep inside.

"I love you too, James."

He'd been gone for about an hour when the nurse came back and checked on me. When she left I turned off the lamp that was screwed into the wall above my hospital bed. I took my pillow and put it in front of my face to muffle the noise. Then I cried. I cried for my baby and a life lost. I cried for my husband. I thought of him at our house, dismantling a crib and putting away baby toys, perhaps even scraping the large letters of the alphabet off the walls of the spare room. And I cried because I knew I wouldn't be able to do it again. I wouldn't go through this again, not for anybody.

## Stephen

I found Billy a couple of days after I returned. After
taking a couple of days off, Myra returned to work and I
checked in with the base at Fort Lewis and asked them to
look him up. He'd been discharged; he was no longer on
active duty, but the army knew where to find him. They
always do, and although the staff sergeant was reluctant to
give me his address, once I told him a little bit about what
happened to us in the ditch, he relented.

I knew his neighborhood. It was on the outside of town.
I'd driven past it many times. I just hadn't expected to find
my friend living there. The bus dropped me at the edge of a
cluster of homes, each sitting on large lots. The mapping
program on my cell phone told me I had a two-mile walk to
his address. This wasn't part of the history I'd imagined
Billy having. I'd double-checked with the bus driver,
asking him if there were any stops closer, but he'd been
sure. It was as though a neighborhood as affluent as this
one didn't need buses. As I walked past the long driveways,
with their manicured hedges, I could see the occupants'
luxury vehicles parked by their front doors. The driver was

right. No buses passed me, and when I looked down the long row of lampposts, there were no bus stops in sight.

The address the sergeant had given me led to a large house in a cul-de-sac. It sat back in a corner, off by itself, and parked outside the front door was a black jeep, raised high off the ground. It looked like an oversized young person's toy. The gate was open so I walked up the drive, trying to picture the image I'd conjured in my head of the wayward man who had no one left in his life. It didn't make sense for him to be living in this lavish home. When I got to the front of the house I looked at the jeep, jacked up in the air, and then at the address on the screen of my cell phone, wondering whether I was at the right place.

"It's air-ride. I push a button and it comes down to the ground, Stephen. That way I can hobble inside."

He was there, silently watching, just like in Afghanistan. He stepped from around the side of the house. As he expertly strode toward me, he stretched his hand out to shake mine. If I hadn't known what had happened, I'd have believed he still had both his legs. When he reached me he put his weight on his bad leg, teetering on it, and took my hand, welcoming me home.

"And look, hand controls. Makes it easier. I've gotten the hang of this thing," he said, smacking the palm of his hand on his artificial leg, "but for driving, especially off-road, the controls take the pressure off."

I stood in his driveway, thousands of miles from where we'd last met, and we avoided speaking about where we'd been and what had happened. Instead, I listened to him as he told me how far into the bush he'd taken his jeep and how he'd had to winch himself out a time or two.

"How did you know I was here? Were you sitting at the window?"

"I have cameras at the entrance, Stephen. I know everything that happens here. Come on. Let's go inside."

The inside of his house was simple and had few furnishings, but the things he did have looked expensive. There was artwork on the walls and small, glass sculptures sitting on little shelves in the main entrance and in the living room. They were the types of things that I ignored in department stores because I knew I couldn't afford them. They looked as though they belonged in a gallery, not in the home of a discharged army corporal.

We talked of men we knew, about how they were doing, and what was happening over there, and he asked how my homecoming with Myra had been.

"It was good. It was the right thing. It feels good to be home."

I wasn't his superior any longer. Our ages mattered more out here, on the outside. There were no stripes or uniforms to tell us apart, and his age and bronzed skin gave him an almost paternal look as he spoke to me.

"I'm glad, Stephen. You deserve to come home to some happiness. You put your time in over there."

We sat in silence for a long moment as I looked around his home, searching for traces of someone else, a photograph, a memory left behind. I could see the reluctance in his face, as though he didn't want to tell me, but after a while, it was like he could sense my questions. He began to open up and started telling me about himself.

"I never told you, but I left school early. I was one of those child geniuses. No, don't laugh, I was. I graduated from college when I was twenty years old, pride of my family. Before me no one had even attended post-secondary school, much less graduated early. I had a job, a car, and a signing bonus before I even threw my cap in the air. I moved north to Redmond, the computer capital, and lived the dot-com company life."

I squinted at him, trying to picture my soldier friend as a computer geek, sitting at a desk.

"I can't see you there, Billy. That doesn't seem like you."

He shook his head and gave me a rare smile.

"That is me, though. That's what got me this place, and for a while, it got me the girl too. Yes, there was a girl. There always is, isn't there?"

I nodded and agreed with him, still trying to reconcile the image of the man in front of me with the man I'd spent time with overseas.

"It was good. Work invigorated me, my wife invigorated me. We moved here, to this house, and everything was going fine. The features you use on that little phone in your pocket, the things you rely on, that's what we created. We could do no wrong. Business was great and I'd come home at night to the girl. It was all good. Until one day, it wasn't."

His dark hair had grown out a little since he'd left Afghanistan, and as he ran his fingers through it, his smile faded. The lost look he had overseas came back, and I began to understand. We were in the hut again, watching the men play cards while he sat in his own personal darkness.

"What happened, Billy? What happened to your wife, your job?"

"I had the wrong girl. I picked the wrong woman. She found the right man for her and it wasn't me. I was somewhere else, working, always working, and after it happened, there was no going back. Nobody wanted to hear about it. Not my family, nobody. When you're flying, when everything is going up they're all there with you, but when it hits the fan, that's when you find out who you can really rely on. When she left, there was nobody there for me. In their eyes I was the one who'd made the mistake. I was the one who hadn't been here when I should have been. They all thought it was my fault, even though she ran off with another man."

In a way, I'd been right. He didn't have anybody. They'd all left him.

"So, I went to the only place where they don't care who you are or where you come from. I knew nobody would ask any questions over there."

It still didn't explain all of it. It didn't make sense. I shook my head as I listened to him telling me his story.

"I don't get it. You get drunk, or you get in a fight, or you go find the girl. You came to hell, you joined up? Why? Didn't you talk to her, or go after her?"

"I didn't want her back. I didn't want anybody. Didn't you hear me? I graduated from college when I was twenty years old. With honors. I headed a department at the largest computer company in the world, and I had this, all of it."

He waved his arms around the large room. He was talking quickly, angry, trying to explain.

"I don't know failure, Stephen. I don't do failure. I never have, but in the end, none of this stuff I created mattered. I had to go somewhere and not be me. My work was always about thinking outside the box. It was time to live outside the box. So, I did."

I know men. I've served with them, lived with them, and sometimes commanded them. I know how they think and what they do, and even a man as unique as Billy has the same trait we all have. He has his pride. I knew he had to have looked for her. We all would have.

"You contacted her though, Billy. You must have? You tried to get her back."

He nodded, thinking about it, I suppose.

"Yes, I found her. I found both of them. And when I told her I was going to Afghanistan she didn't care. She knows me. She knows that when I say I'm going to do something, I do it. She didn't care enough. Like I said, she was the wrong girl."

We all have our stories—our pains, our burdens—and Billy, in his rich-man's house, had his. He followed through on a threat and it cost him his leg. Everyone left him alone, and he got used to it, tucked away in the darkness of his big house. I wasn't going to do that. I couldn't.

He drove me all the way back into town and pulled up outside Myra's supermarket. As we sat in his jeep, with the engine running, he forced a strained smile onto his dark, sad face.

"I'm sure she's a great girl, your Myra. Hold on to her. Don't listen to me and my miserable story. You're going to be fine."

He lowered the airbags. The vehicle dropped close to the ground, and I jumped out. Before he could pull away, I put my head back inside the door.

"You'll have Christmas dinner with us. Christmas Day, couple of days from now, I'll be in touch."

"I don't think I will, Stephen."

"It wasn't a request, Corporal, I'll see you for Christmas dinner. Thanks for the ride."

I didn't wait for him to answer. I'd been in the ditch with him. I'd made a decision that cost him, and I wasn't going to leave him the way everyone else had. I closed the door behind me and watched him drive away before heading to the back of the store to pick up my wife.

Becky

I needed to stay busy. I had to, so I went back to work almost immediately. During my absence, the museum hired a new ticket-taker and he seemed to enjoy doing what I hadn't, so my previous position was filled. Fortunately, there was an opening that seemed more promising. The manager of procurements needed an assistant. My qualifications didn't make me a natural candidate, but I impressed the board enough that they decided to give me the job. My career giving change from twenty-dollar bills was over, and I couldn't have been happier.

I enjoyed my new job. My manager was a kind old soul who was counting the days until his retirement, and he let me have more of a free rein than he probably should have. With a little guidance from him, I had input into which exhibitions we should be pursuing, and I was able to decide which displays should be highlighted. I felt as though my career was just beginning, and I was finally able to utilize some of the knowledge and training that my parents had invested in.

For a few hours each day I buried my mind in colors and shapes and ideas that had nothing to do with what had happened. And most days, things got a little better. The memory of the pain, the actual physical pain, eases itself from your mind quickly. I knew I'd gone through months of discomfort and upset stomachs. There were days when it had been pure agony, but I couldn't feel it anymore; that part was gone. Emotional pain is different though. That takes longer to heal, and sometimes I suppose it never does.

There were elements that made me remember, and it wasn't always the obvious things. I'd drive to work and see women or men pushing strollers. Or, I'd see small children walking to school. I was happy for them. I imagined them living safe, warm lives and experiencing things together, as a family. That wasn't what brought the hurt back. The hurt came when I'd see the look on his face. Sometimes, when he didn't realize I was watching, I'd glance over and there was no smile, no sparkling blue eyes. It didn't matter how hard he tried to hide it—I knew it was there. It was the look that said I'd let him down.

James says that the area we live in is as large as some countries, and he's probably right. Seattle, Tacoma, and even some of the towns that surround those cities are infamous for their traffic jams. In order to drive anywhere you have to time it very carefully, because gridlock on the highways can delay you for hours. James had work obligations that took him all over both cities and even further afield. The tasks he'd previously been able to manage from home kept him away at the office, and the calls he'd been able to make from our home phone were no longer sufficient. Now he preferred to visit his clients in person. He'd call me from the road and explain that he was stuck with a customer or that there was an accident and traffic was backed up. He'd tell me that he might as well eat dinner out by himself or skip it altogether. Our weekends were often disrupted too. Work that he wasn't able to attend to during the week had to be dealt with on Saturdays or even Sundays. He had no choice.

While James was building his wholesale division, I spent evenings with my parents, and when I tired of that, I worked extra hours at the museum. Then I'd come home late, eat by myself, and wait for him. That's what we'd become: two people loving each other, eating alone. I've heard it said that the most precious commodity we have is our time. I never realized how true that was until it was the one thing I couldn't get from him.

On the few nights when we managed to coordinate our schedules, I'd plan our meals in advance, hoping we'd be able to spend a couple of hours together. Sometimes it worked. I'd cook and try to make everything just the way it was before. We'd sit and visit, and eat. He'd tell me about contracts he'd secured or deals he'd made, and I'd try to interest him in the sculptures from the Middle East that I was trying to bring to the museum. We were polite and kind, and we loved each other. I know we did.

That became our lives. A year can pass, even longer, with nothing happening. I know it can, because I lived through it. I lived through occasional dinners at my parents' home or at our apartment. I lived through the infrequent nights when we'd go to the movies, and hold hands. Those were the good nights. And I lived through the canceled dinners and long evenings and weekends when he was working. For a whole year the same things happened over and over, and I accepted them; it felt normal. Christmas came and went. The time of year when he proposed to me was also the time of year when we'd suffered our loss. It had once been so special to us, but we allowed it to become just another holiday. I decorated a tree while he worked late, and then we ate turkey dinner at my parents' home; we even watched a Christmas movie on television. It never felt like Christmas though. It was never like the Christmases he'd promised me or the Christmases we'd dreamed about.

Some days I marveled at how fast time went by. We'd look out our apartment window at the city and talk about how green everything was from the rain, or we'd complain about the wet streets or that the traffic was bad. They were the same conversations we'd had our whole lives, yet we talked about them as though it was something we'd just discovered. We just kept on living, trying to pretend everything was okay.

After a while, I could tell that boredom set in for him, and he wasn't able to shake it off. He'd never get angry with anyone or even frustrated, but he had a new look in his eyes, a look that wasn't there before. Our infrequent dinners, and the time we managed to spend together, would be too neat, too uneventful. There was always something missing.

Sometimes we made love. He'd tell me I was beautiful and stroke my hair and touch my body, and then afterward he'd turn away and lay by himself. I knew he was hurting; we both were. It doesn't go away, but I needed more. We probably both did. We lay in bed and I listened to him breathing, sorting through his own thoughts.

"I'm sorry, James. I'm sorry, but I just can't try again, not yet."

At first he said nothing. Then, his voice came. Not the confident sales executive voice and not the voice of the college student I fell in love with—just a voice that I suppose he always had.

"It's fine, Becky, it's not that. Things are going to get better. I promise you they will. I promise."

Then, he'd reach over and touch me for a moment. He'd stroke my side, or the tips of his fingers would glance against the back of my hand, but he'd never turn around, and he never held me.

On the day he stopped promising that it was going to get better, I knew things had gone too far. We made love, and afterward he just lay there, turned away from me, not talking. I asked him what I could do, and then I waited for him to make his promise to me, the way he always did. This time he didn't though. Finally, I heard his breathing change and I knew he'd fallen asleep.

There was too much distance between us. It had become unbearable. Physically he changed too. He had no appetite and he was losing weight. He was wearing himself out, working nights, weekends, and he wouldn't let me help carry the burden. He should have let me. We should have moved, changed apartments, changed jobs, gone away, done something, anything. I couldn't take it anymore. It had been almost two years since we lost our baby. December approached again, another Christmas that neither of us was ready to acknowledge. If we were going to resurrect our marriage, this had to be the time to do it.

I made him promise me that he'd take a Sunday off work, and I packed a picnic lunch and loaded it into the trunk of our car.

I don't think he knew where we were going, not at first anyway. It was just nice to have him with me and be present for once.

"It's a cold day to be traipsing around, Becky. Are we going Christmas shopping? It's early for that."

He was a different man. Instead of the grin that I had fallen in love with, the corners of his mouth dropped, and he had a sad, resigned look on his face.

"I told you, it's a surprise."

After a while the realization set in and he nodded to himself. He knew where we were headed as I drove our little car out to the only place I knew that might still save us.

"You don't have to take us there, Becky. It's fine. It's cold and it's the wrong time of year."

I ignored him and looked forward, thinking about a December where I'd told him the same thing and how he managed to change my mind. I held on to the steering wheel, trying to believe that my plan would work.

It was still there; it hadn't changed. Treshingham had the same ugly, grey, beautiful pallor to it. Its mysterious name was still forged onto the large wall on the side, and around the building little tufts of grass poked through the blacktop of the old parking lot. I looked at the row of old doors lined up along the back, and focused on the one he'd kicked open for me.

"Feel like kicking in any doors today, honey?"

"Becky…"

I wouldn't accept anything less than everything. I wanted him back; I wanted us back. I got out of the car and pulled the picnic basket from the trunk. Then, I awkwardly laid it on the small console between our seats.

"Your mom's car had more room. Don't spill."

His face was white, and he looked uncomfortable. He wanted it to stop. I could tell, but I wouldn't accept that.

"Becky, you shouldn't have done all this."

I wouldn't look at him and his disapproval, his unwillingness to try.

"Eat. Here, James, have a sandwich. Please take a sandwich."

I didn't look up. I just kept my gaze on the basket as I handed him a wrapped sandwich. I'd made it on the wheat germ bread with rosemary that he loved so much, and I'd picked up the spread that he liked, from the specialty store on the other side of the city. It was perfect. He took the sandwich and put it on the dash in front of him. Then he looked out the window for a long time. He was shaking as he stared out at Treshingham.

I pulled my sandwich from the basket and took a bite, trying to swallow it past the lump in my throat. This was my life. I would not give up.

"I love you, James. I love you."

Then, he said the words that nobody should have to hear when they're trying so hard. "Becky, we need to talk. There's something I need to tell you."

His face turned whiter, paler. His breathing was labored. Still staring out the front window, he wiped the sweat from his brow.

"James, it's okay. Take it easy."

I put my sandwich down and reached over the basket toward him. He was gasping for air, and the sound of his heavy, inconsistent breaths filled the car. He leaned forward and back again, trying to catch his breath.

"James, what's happening to you? Stop it, honey. You're scaring me."

Then, he slumped forward and his head hit the dashboard.

Stephen

Billy had Christmas dinner with us. I didn't give him a choice. My sister and her family took their kids to Mike's parents' home for their annual feast, so it was just the three of us. We'd been invited to join my sister, and Myra wanted to go, but I wanted to spend our first Christmas in our own house and after some playful negotiation, she relented.

Before he arrived I told her a little about what had happened in Afghanistan, but only a little. She knew that Billy had lost his leg in a combat situation, but that was all. The rest of the story was his and mine. There was no need for her to hear any more than she had to.

We met him at the door, together. She was tucked in behind me, sheltering herself from the cold. It was hard to believe that just over a week ago I'd been in a different country, and now I was home with my wife standing beside me. I felt like two parts of my life were coming together. He stood on his artificial leg, balancing slightly on one side, and looked warily at Myra. It felt like he was trying to decide whether or not to come in.

"You made it. Good, come in, come in. This is my wife, Myra."

She was wearing her apron, covered in flour, and a bright red sweater that I'd given her for Christmas. Her long hair was tied behind her head, and she appraised him the same way she inspected me the first time we met.

"Two soldiers for Christmas. I'm a lucky girl."

Billy seemed lost for words. They watched each other for a moment before he broke the silence and shook her hand, thanking us for having him. Then, just as suddenly as she'd appeared, she disappeared back to the kitchen and left us, calling back to me.

"Close that door, Stephen; you'll let the heat out."

And, like generations of men before me, I shrugged, smiled, and took my friend's jacket as he followed me into our house.

It was a lot of work for her. I hadn't been home long, and I was bringing a stranger into our house, but she did it. She made turkey, and cranberry sauce, and potatoes, and she baked an apple pie for dessert. She told us that one of the few useful things her mother had taught her as she was growing up was how to make a homemade apple pie. She'd taught her well. I'd never tasted such a good pie.

Our conversation was polite but distant. Myra and Billy didn't seem to hit it off right away. It wasn't that she disliked him, or he disliked her. They just didn't seem to have anything to say to each other. Her flirty gestures and good-natured jests didn't work on him. He didn't sulk; he was too far into his own darkness to give any woman— even my wife—any type of positive energy.

He didn't want to stay. I knew he didn't want to be there. When dinner ended, he tried to leave but got caught up in the whirlwind of kids when my niece and nephew arrived. Their dinner with Mike's family had finished early, and they dropped by to visit. The kids ran through the doorway and then raced from room to room in our small house, playing with their Christmas toys and burning off the dinners they'd eaten. As they almost bowled him over, Billy grinned, and it was the happiest I'd seen him.

After I hurriedly introduced him to everyone Allyson made her apologies, as she chased after my niece and nephew.

"I'm sorry. They had too much sugar earlier today. They're not usually like this."

I put the palm of my hand to my mouth, as though I were telling him a secret.

"It's a lie, Billy. Don't let her fool you. They're always like this."

One of them shrieked as a toy was grabbed. Tears would follow, and by the end of the day they'd hug and console each other. It's the way it had been with my sister and me, and it was the same way with her children.

I flinched as the sounds of their playing and squealing filled our previously quiet house. Billy didn't move though. He just kept grinning.

"That's the healthiest sound in the world, Stephen. There's nothing like it."

Mike rushed by, on his way to help his wife sort out the latest disagreement, and Myra appeared from the kitchen, smiling, agreeing with my friend.

"I like that. You're right, Billy. That is a healthy sound."

It was a good way to end his visit. My wife and my friend agreed with each other. After he left, she never talked about how sad he looked, or asked me any questions, and I appreciated that.

My days of combat were over. I took a desk job and gained a little weight. It often happens. We come back from overseas, become too attached to our partners' home cooking, and we add a couple of extra pounds. Myra brought home food from her supermarket, and we ate very well. Some nights, I barbecued steaks on the grill in our backyard, or she cooked Italian food on the old stove. Our life together became regular. We made plans. We talked about my leaving the service and getting a job in the civilian-workforce that paid a little more, or maybe buying a house or taking a trip, and all the while we tried to make a baby. We both wanted to start a family.

Nothing changed for Billy. He worked from home and consulted for an Internet company. He seemed to enjoy it, and his darkness would disappear from time to time, but it never really went away. I'd meet him at one of the coffee shops in the city, or he'd pick me up and we'd hang out at his house and talk while we installed the latest accessory he'd purchased for his jeep. His health was good, and he got around well on his artificial leg, but there didn't seem to be any joy in his life as he sat alone in his big house. The little flashes of light that came into his eyes never lasted for very long.

The months went by and the kids got bigger. My nephew started school, and my niece cried all day until he came home. Myra got a promotion, helping out in the warehouse instead of standing at a cash register all day. And I shuffled papers at my desk or sat in meetings, learning about organization and delegation within the military. Our life was quiet, but it was good. The weeks and months passed at their own pace. The clock that had hung so prominently over our heads before I left for Afghanistan disappeared. Christmas came again, and Billy paid his annual visit to our house. He hadn't seen Myra since the previous Christmas, and although she tried her same friendly, flirtatious routine on him, he still didn't buy into it. They were polite to each other, but nothing else was there. Again, he waited until the children arrived so he could see them, and hear them. And then he left and went home to his big house.

We did the things normal people do. We dreamed and talked and lived, and all the while, Myra and I kept trying to start a family. We talked about my niece and nephew, and other children we knew. I kept hoping she was going to reveal the secret to me and tell me she was carrying our child, but it never happened. After a while, we made love less often. We settled into a routine, in the same way that most couples do I suppose, but it was still good. We still enjoyed the intimacy we had with each other. The baby just never came, and the question was always there, hanging. I needed to know, and one day I asked her.

"Should we see someone, a doctor? Maybe there's something they can suggest."

I was putting on my uniform, getting ready for work. It was a day when our schedules didn't mesh. She had a day off and was spending it at home while I was at base. She knew what I meant. I know she must have been thinking about it too. At first she didn't answer me. She stayed sitting in bed, leafing through her magazine.

"Maybe it's my positioning. Maybe there's something new we can try."

I stood at the door grinning, waiting until she laid her magazine on her lap and looked up at me.

"It'll happen, Stephen. Just give it some time."

I'd never been married before or lived with a woman. The only examples I had of couples in healthy relationships were my parents while they were still with us, and my sister and her husband. I tried to do what I'd seen them doing. I worked hard at the base, did chores around our old house, and I tried to be a good husband. Everything was good, but we had a plan, and I was tired of waiting for it to happen.

She stared at me, her hair hanging sleepily on her shoulders, and then she gave me her crooked smile.

"Let's just try and enjoy it, Stephen. Don't you enjoy me anymore?"

She knew I did. Our marriage had been hurried, and then I left her for a whole year. It must have been like having an imaginary husband. Then, suddenly I was home every day. And, almost two years later, some days it felt like we were still getting to know each other. The adjustment hadn't been fair to her. I knew she was trying her best.

"Yes, I enjoy you, Mrs. Brown. You know I do."

That was all it took. The discussion ended again, and I let it go. I accepted the fact that it hadn't happened yet. She was right; it didn't matter. We were young, we had time, and nothing was perfect. Like any young couple we had our good days and our bad days. On the good days it felt like we were together and striving for something. But, on the bad days, it seemed as though the normalcy of our life was getting to her. I could hear it in her voice, see it in her indifference. She would fade away, and there was nothing I could do to bring her back. I let her have her space, her own interests. I had the time I spent with Billy, and I still enjoyed the evenings when I looked after my niece and nephew. And she had her television shows and the long phone conversations with her girlfriends. It seemed like everything was okay. It was the way it should be.

I'm told that if you look back and analyze a relationship, you can pinpoint the exact time when it went wrong. That's probably true. We certainly had our moment. Maybe it was there all along and I didn't see it. Maybe I was working too hard to keep the wheels spinning, trying to create what I wanted, and I didn't see the signs even though they were right in front of me.

We spent an evening at Allyson and Mike's. It was early December and we were planning gifts, dinners. With the talk of presents and Santa Claus, the children were on their best behavior. They sat and listened to us. Occasionally they laughed out loud or teased each other, but with Santa's visit looming, they were as quiet as I'd ever seen them. Allyson was running around as usual, taking pots off the stove, trying to find the remote for the television so she could turn it off, and talking all the time. Their work relationship had changed. With Myra's promotion she'd become part of the warehouse staff while Allyson still spent her days standing at the check-out in the supermarket, so the two of them didn't see each other as frequently as they once had. They weren't especially close, but like many people who work together, when they socialized they had lots to talk about. Allyson reeled off names of workmates Mike and I didn't know. She mentioned names or situations and we'd shrug at each other, offering comments from time to time, trying to throw my sister off her stories.

"Mike, I think that one was sick with gout last time we heard this. Or did she have a new hairdresser? I don't remember now, do you?"

He fired back immediately.

"Hairdresser, Stephen. She was going with a new color. I remember because last time when they talked about her I couldn't sleep all night. I tossed and turned worrying that everything was going to be okay with her hair."

My sister threw a dish towel at her husband. I felt it flying past my head as the children let out whoops of laughter.

"Enough, you two. I don't get to do this anymore. Let me catch Myra up on what she's missing. I'm not allowed to associate with these warehouse people, you know."

Myra chortled. She was happy, enjoying herself for once. And, then just as quickly as it began, it ended. Allyson said a name, the name of someone they both knew, and everything changed. It was just a name. It should have meant nothing. But when she heard it Myra covered her mouth with her hand and sucked in her breath.

"No. No."

She stood up, knocking her chair backward, and everything was quiet. Even the children didn't speak. I got up and walked toward her, wanting to help.

"What is it, honey? What's wrong?"

The pupils of her eyes were tiny. She was shaking, looking at me.

"Don't. I need to go. I need to go see him."

That was the moment. That was when everything in my life changed.

# Becky

I didn't panic. I cried, but I didn't panic. Through my tears, I kept talking to him. I told him he was going to be okay, and I called the emergency number on my cell phone. The operator told me what to do and in the process gave me the answer to our long-ago mystery."Treshingham? Is that where you are? You're at the old hospital now. You're very close. I've dispatched an ambulance, but it'll be faster if you can drive. Listen to me carefully, is he breathing? Is he conscious?"

He was and when I pulled him back in the seat his eyes opened. He wasn't quite with me, but his breaths were steadier than they had been before he hit his head. I strained my eyes, trying to see through my tears. Then I quickly pulled away from Treshingham, and followed the man's directions.

I called our parents, my mom and dad, and James's folks, and they must have driven like they were on rocket ships because they arrived almost right away. James's mother tried to take charge, asking the nurses questions and demanding to speak to a doctor. There was nothing they could do to help her though. The nurses didn't know. They'd taken James into an operating room when we arrived and told me to wait. So, I waited. When our parents got there we all waited, and worried. None of us had any answers.

When the doctor finally appeared she was moving quickly, searching the faces in the waiting room, calling my name.

"You need to come with me, Rebecca. He's going to see you, all of you, but you need to come first. We only need the wife for now please."

James's mother stood up right away, but the doctor put her hand up and held her back. I followed her along the hallway, walking on the little colored feet that were on the floor.

She told me he was resting and his vitals were stable, and that was when I started to panic. I kept thinking that it had been nothing. He'd hit his head, that was all. I sucked in three sharp, deep breaths in a row and stumbled along beside her, barely keeping up.

"It's okay. Keep coming, Rebecca. Follow me."

She didn't try to help me. She just kept walking her long, quick strides, urging me along. We passed through a large set of glass doors, and she asked me about his diet and whether he was under any stress, and then she nodded her head, mentally recording my answers. All the time, she kept her lips pursed, listening, making sure I was keeping up with her. She said more. I know she did, and I listened to it all, but the one thing she never said was that he was going to be okay. Not once.

He had tubes coming from his arm and his nose, and he had a red mark on his forehead between his eyes where he'd hit the dashboard. There was a monitor over his bed making little chirping noises as lights flashed across the screen. A nurse was beside him, adjusting hoses, watching him. When we walked into the room, the doctor touched the nurse on the arm, hurrying her along, dismissing her.

"Your husband had a mild heart attack before you brought him here."

It didn't make sense. None of it. He couldn't have had a heart attack while we sat in the car at Treshingham. It wasn't possible.

"He hit his head. He just hit his head and he couldn't breathe."

The doctor nodded, agreeing, as though she'd been there with us.

"It's good that he hit his head. That probably saved him. It brought his breathing back under control, but when we admitted him he had another attack, a more severe one. This is serious, Rebecca. If he doesn't stabilize soon, we're going to have to operate."

I looked at my husband, at the monitor, at the hoses.

"No, no, no. Doctor, something is wrong here. This isn't possible. He's young. His heart is fine; it has to be. We're young, this can't be happening."

She nodded impatiently, as though she didn't want to explain it to me.

"Heart failure can happen to anyone, anytime. I'm sorry, but we need to get him through this, and then we can talk about what happened. The next few hours are very important. We need to keep him stable. Sit with him, Rebecca. Sit with him and talk to him. You're right. He's young and strong. Talk him through this, and bring him back."

Then she left us. The nurse left too, and moved to the other side of the glass door, telling me that if anything happened it would record on her monitor. And, if I needed her, I just had to call, or knock on the glass. It seemed like five minutes ago we'd been driving out to Treshingham and five minutes before that we'd been asleep at home, in our bed. None of this should have been happening.

I sat with him, and then they let his parents come in, and then my parents. They came into the room two at a time, whispering, talking to him, and encouraging him. His eyes quickly opened for a brief moment, and he seemed to acknowledge us. I held on to his mother and we cried together. Then, he smiled; I'm sure he did. The corner of his mouth curled up and he smiled at me, loving me, and then his eyes closed again.

A day passed, a whole day, and the last thing that mattered to me was his work. I didn't care about it, but I did what had to be done. I asked my father to call his office so they could alert all the food places that he wouldn't be coming to see them or getting calls from him. And we watched him and waited, hoping the beats on the monitor would get stronger, closer together. I fell asleep in the chair for a few minutes, and then woke up, chastising myself for dozing off.

The doctor came back and made notes on a pad that hung on a clipboard at the end of the bed. She could have written anything she liked; I didn't understand any of it. The curtains were closed around the glass walls of the room. The only light was from the monitor over his bed, and the only sounds were the beeping and his breathing. His chest slowly went up and back down. Little puffs of air came from his mouth, in and out, never stronger, never faster.

His mother sat on one side of his bed and I on the other while his father and my parents visited for a few moments and then left again. The owner of the food company that he worked for came, but the nurse wouldn't let him in. I went to the outer room to see him and he held on to me as though he knew me well. He told me how strong James was and how much he respected him. Then before he left, he told me that he'd had an uncle who battled through heart disease. Others came—friends and workmates. I didn't know most of them. In just over forty-eight hours there were an endless amount of faces watching him from the other side of the glass, not being allowed in. I could hear their muffled conversations as they talked about relatives who'd battled cancers or other deadly ailments. I didn't care. It didn't matter. This was my husband. I didn't want to hear their stories of survivals and failures. This was my life, not theirs. I shook my head as I listened, questioning the relevance of their tales, wishing they would all go away. When they finally went, and I was left with the beeping and breathing, and the soft sobs of his mother on the other side of the bed, I thought about their whispers. Maybe they were right. Disease is disease and mortality is mortality. It doesn't matter what tries to take our life from us. The question is whether we're able to battle back and fight it. He was strong. He'd battle back. I knew he would.

He became a little more conscious the next morning. I don't know what time it was but it was morning, I knew that much. He came back to us, and for a moment it was as though he'd been sleeping. He was weak, but he was with us and he was getting better. His eyes flickered open, and then they stayed open, and finally, they darted around. He didn't move his head, but his eyes looked around, and he was more aware. That's when I knocked on the door, calling for help. His mother stepped back from the bed, forcing herself to give the doctor room, afraid perhaps that she'd be asked to leave.

The doctor checked the readings on the monitor, and then took a small light and shone it in his eyes trying to get him to react.

"James, can you hear me? Do you know where you are, James?"

It was the friendliest I'd seen her. I wanted to tell her that he couldn't answer while he had a tube in his mouth, but I didn't. She knew what she was doing.

At first nothing happened, and then the little muscles in his face began to twitch as he strained to speak. The hose in his mouth moved, and he got a word out. It sounded like "good." It probably was. He was trying to tell us he was okay.

One whole day can mean a lot. He started to show signs of improvement. Little bits of him came back. We spoke to him about positive things. His mother told him they were having us over for Christmas dinner later in the month. This year it was their turn, and it was non-negotiable. She promised him there would be no brussels sprouts and then waited for a reaction. When it didn't come she did the right thing. She kept talking, being positive, and helping. His father and my dad told him how proud they were of him. They talked about how they enjoyed hearing about his sales conquests, and that they were starved for more tales of deals being brokered and contracts being signed. And I told him I loved him. It's all I could do. It was all I had.

In one of the few moments when no one else was in the room I leaned forward and whispered to him.

"Nothing matters, honey. Nothing. Whatever is going on we'll get through it. We'll come out the other side of this thing and you'll be stronger. We'll both be stronger."

His eyes opened and then closed again, and the little lights on the monitor kept beeping and flashing.

After another day he could almost speak. His strength was coming back slowly, little by little. It was our fourth day in the hospital, and he seemed to be getting better. He made little words, and he could form garbled sentences. His mother or my mother would lean over him, trying to hear a little more, and in a faint, almost unintelligible voice he told them he loved them. Their reaction was the same. They touched him gently, not wanting to disturb the equipment that was strapped to him, and then they stepped back and teared up, having faith, believing that he was going to be okay. When he was finally able to move his head around a little, he waited until they all left the room. Then he tilted forward and motioned for me to come closer, and in between shallow, weak breaths, he said the words I didn't want to hear.

"Becky. Becky. Just in case…"

I wouldn't accept it. There would be no "just in case." I leaned back from him. I was gentle but firm, and I would not let him finish.

"No, honey. That's not going to happen. You're going to be fine. We're going to celebrate Christmas together soon. Remember, James, you told me we'd have lots of Christmases together, and we will. We will, honey."

He looked up at me. His face didn't move, only his eyes. His eyes were deciding. I held his gaze, loving him, but daring him to continue. I didn't want to know anything. I didn't want to know what he'd been trying to tell me in the car. I didn't want Treshingham to be an old hospital, and I didn't want my husband to be lying in a bed with a machine beeping above him.

It took him a few moments, and then, as though he'd made a decision, he closed his eyes and opened them again, loving me back.

On the fifth day my husband had another heart attack. They say that a minor heart attack is an attack that you live through. James's attack on the fifth day was not minor, and he did not come back to us. His monitor slowed and the little puffs of breath slowly, urgently, escaped from his mouth. A different doctor rushed in and then another, along with nurses and orderlies. They pushed us away from his bed and did what they could to try to save him. Nothing helped. His mother and I held each other tight and watched as the little puffs of air from his mouth slowed down and then stopped. All their equipment and expertise and good intentions couldn't help him. His body shut down. They told me what happened. He had a congenital heart defect. It was a medical term I didn't care about. All that mattered to me was that there would be no more Christmases for us. James left me, and he took my heart with him.

# Stephen

The door slammed shut behind her as she ran out. For one long moment none of us moved. I suppose we were probably in shock. Allyson didn't know what had happened, it was so quick, and so unexpected. By the time I got to the street there was no sign of her. I ran the few blocks to our house. I thought I'd catch her as she was walking along the sidewalk, but she wasn't there. It didn't make sense. Nothing made sense. We had been sitting around the table, laughing. Allyson spoke of coworkers and then mentioned the name of a salesman from one of the companies that did business with the supermarket. He was ill, and in the hospital; something was wrong with his heart. She said things didn't look good for him. I didn't understand. Did Myra know him? Had she dealt with him? I walked through our house, from room to room, but it was empty. She hadn't come home.

I looked into our bedroom. The bed was unmade and one of her magazines lay on the bedside table. The living room was empty. I went into the bathroom. Everything was the same way it always was. The only thing missing was my wife.

I called her cell phone. It rang once and went to voice mail. I paced back and forth across the living room floor. I put my face to the glass and strained to see out the window. I walked back into the street and stared up and down the road, trying to find her. I went into our bedroom and opened her closet. All of her things were there: her jeans hanging side by side, blouses, the dress she wore when we married. There was nothing to see, nothing out of place. I'd never opened her dresser drawers or looked at her things. They weren't my business, but I was desperate. I had to. I opened the small drawer at the side of her bed. Inside was a small notebook, another magazine, and a necklace. I fingered the notebook. Her girlfriends' phone numbers might be in the book. I didn't know any of them. They were just names and voices on the telephone. She hadn't invited them to the house while I was home, but I could call their numbers and ask if they'd heard from her. I couldn't do it. I tossed the book on the bed, deciding to leave it alone.

I moved to the bathroom. I kept my shaving accessories in a small cupboard above the sink. I'd given Myra the large one below the vanity, but I'd never had any reason to go into it. I bent down and opened it. There were toiletries, a compact, and tucked in behind them was a blister package of pills. I pulled it out. The days of the week were marked beside each pill. Some were missing and some were still in the package. I'd seen birth control pills before. I knew what they looked like. I held it in my hand, wondering why, trying to understand.

When my cell phone rang I jumped, and it scared me as much as any explosion in Afghanistan. I didn't look at the name. I just pushed the button, hoping it was her.

"Stephen, it's Ally. Is she there?"

"No, she isn't here. I need to find her. Do you know why she'd have birth control pills here, Allyson? Why would she be using birth control pills?"

There was a long pause. My sister was having one of her conversations in her head. I knew she was, but I had no patience for it this time. I paced back and forth, gripping the phone in my hand.

"Stephen, I called a woman I know who works in the warehouse with Myra. Honey, there's something you need to know. The man I talked about, the man who's in the hospital, Myra knows him. Apparently she knows him really well."

"No, Allyson. Don't tell me this. Don't say it."

"I'm sorry, honey. No one told me. Only a couple of them knew. Apparently it's been going on for a while. The woman said she thinks they've been meeting up during the day on Myra's days off. Stephen…"

I didn't want to hear any more. I hung up the phone as my sister continued to say my name. Now I could understand my wife's coldness, her boredom. I walked around the living room, looking at the furniture, remembering. I squeezed my cell phone, resisting the urge to throw it against the wall. Sometimes, on the days when she was off work she'd call me, asking me where I was, confirming that I was still at the base, miles away. I walked into the kitchen, remembering how she'd teased me by bending over the cupboards the day I came back from overseas. I couldn't bear to think about it anymore. I walked past the bathroom. I remembered coming home one afternoon a little early, finding her in the bathtub. She was shocked to see me, frightened almost. Maybe he'd just left. Maybe they'd spent time together in our bathtub, in our house.

I needed to know what it was. Was it love or sex, or boredom? She had run away, to the hospital to see him I suppose, so it must have been more than sex. It had to have been. Or, maybe I was wrong. I needed to talk to her, to ask her why. I needed her to tell me that it was all wrong and that nothing had happened.

When the door opened I thought she was coming back. Maybe there was hope.

Allyson looked at the disarray, the opened doors and drawers. She held me, but I pushed her away. I didn't want that. I wanted to be angry. I didn't want to be the soldier at the airport walking around trouble any more. This was different; this was my wife. I wanted questions answered. I wanted none of it to have ever happened.

"Stay at our place. Don't be here tonight. Let her do what she has to do and then talk it out in the morning. It's for the best."

"Who is he, Ally? Where is he?"

"He's just a guy, just a man. He's not well. He had some kind of a heart attack, and he's out at the hospital in Auburn. The manager from the supermarket went to see him, and it's not looking good for him. And, Stephen, you should know, he's married too. His wife will be at the hospital with him."

You can't be angry with someone who's dying. You can't. It isn't possible. I shook my head and paced around our living room. Allyson was over the initial shock, but she couldn't understand why she hadn't known. She thought she'd failed me.

"I can't believe nobody told me. They were very good at keeping this a secret, Stephen."

I sat on the edge of the sofa that had once been in the basement apartment of her parents' home and probably was in the house she shared with her boyfriend before that. It didn't feel right anymore. One name had been spoken and everything changed. It didn't feel like our home, and I didn't want to be there. I took a deep breath and surprised myself by speaking quietly, calmly.

"It's not your fault. You're right. I won't go to the hospital. And, I don't want to see her tonight even if she does come back. I'll deal with it tomorrow, all of it."

I couldn't stay at my sister's house, so I went to the only other place I had. The entrance to Billy's driveway was closed when we drove up, but he must have recognized us, and the electronic gate swung open right away. Ally dropped me and my duffel bag at his front door. He didn't seem surprised, and he didn't ask why. He just saw me with my things and said that it was okay, and then we waved at my sister as she drove back down his driveway.

The next day came and went, and I decided I didn't want to see her right away. I commuted from Billy's to the base and didn't miss a day of work. When the bus passed the stop where I'd usually get off for our house, I kept staring out the window, trying to sort out my thoughts. At Allyson's supermarket, the floodgates opened, and the information poured freely. All the secrets that hadn't been talked about suddenly became very obvious. My sister reprimanded half the staff she worked with or the ones she thought might have known. She couldn't accept that no one had told her. They knew she was Myra's sister-in-law, yet they managed to conceal the fact that one of the women who worked in the warehouse was having an affair with a sales representative. Once that secret was out all bets were off. All the women wanted to give their reasons why they hadn't told her, and they couldn't wait to give their version now that everybody knew.

I'm sure that some of it was conjecture, but most of it was true; it had to be. It had been going on for some months. They started flirting, much the same way Myra did with the construction workers next door or with almost any man she interacted with. He was a lost soul, problems with his marriage had been mentioned, and he'd taken the bait. He visited the store at all hours, spending time with her. Then, eventually, he didn't come to the store at all. Myra had shared with a girlfriend that he came to see her on her days off, and the girlfriend spilled the beans to Allyson. That's how they managed to spend time together. I had been right about that part. He'd been in our home. Then the man passed away. He had a weak heart. I don't know if his wife found out. The women at the store didn't know her and couldn't answer that question. And I didn't know if Myra loved him. None of the gossip would tell me that.

Billy was happy to let me stay at his place, and he seemed glad to have some company. He didn't talk about what had happened to him or make comparisons. He just told me I deserved to be happy, and that I had to decide whether or not she was the right girl. In his opinion, that was the only important thing. When I was ready to see her, he loaned me his oversized jeep, and I drove through the city and back to our house. I parked outside, waiting until I saw movement in the living room window. She was there, her tall, slender figure moving around.

She didn't look surprised to see me. Allyson had told me that she hadn't gone back to work, so I'd given her some time. It had been a week, a long week.

"I thought you'd come sooner."

She looked at me lazily and spoke slowly. She looked tired, as though she hadn't slept in a while.

"I needed to think, Myra."

We were civilized. We moved into the kitchen, and I pulled out one of our dining room chairs and she took another, sitting at the opposite side of our small table from me.

For a while we said nothing. I stared out the window, watching the old tree leaning against the house. When I finally met her gaze she had a defiant look on her face, and when she apologized it was brief and without remorse.

"I'm sorry, Stephen. I'm sorry this has happened to you."

There was no accountability, no guilt.

"Did you love him?"

She shook her head, impatient with me, as though she was refusing to answer.

"Was it something I did? I don't get it. Did you love him, Myra? I need to know."

She was in a daze, somewhere else, oblivious to my feelings.

"Maybe. I'll never know. He's gone. I was at the hospital, you know. I was there when he died."

I didn't want to hear it. All I wanted was for her to feel the hurt as much as I did.

"Was his wife there, Myra? What did she think of you being there? Was she good with it all?"

Then, she gave me a little bit. And I began to understand. This had been her out. She didn't want me. She didn't want any of it.

"You don't understand, Stephen. This isn't me. This house, us, it isn't for me and it probably never was. I thought it was when we met. I thought when we got together you were what I wanted. You were my big, handsome soldier. It's not though. Maybe I don't know what I want. Maybe it wasn't him either."

She looked up at me, pleading almost. "It's not your fault, and it wasn't hers either. Nothing was. It just happened."

"You didn't answer me. Does she know?"

She changed the subject, still not wanting to own what she had done.

"Stephen, you need to decide what you're going to do. Your things are here, what do you want me to do with them? I'm moving back in with my folks. My dad knows a lawyer. We can get a divorce easily. Let's just get it over with, Stephen."

She didn't know. The man's wife didn't know about the affair. Myra's colors were shining through, and I didn't feel anything for her any more. She didn't want a family and she never had. She didn't want any of the things I wanted.

It had all been a fantasy. We were over, but the man's wife had a right. She had a right to know what had happened.

## Becky

At first you're in a fog, and then, when it lifts, you become a pedestrian. You can see everything around you happening, but you don't feel as though you're participating. You're just an observer, standing back, watching. Before it happened, I never had the thoughts that some people say they have. I never wondered what it would be like to not have my husband around. I always assumed that forever meant forever. So, when I lost James, I didn't know what to do. I didn't want to start over. I didn't want to leave that hospital without him. And, most of all, I didn't want him to be dead. It was as simple as that.

That first night I wouldn't go with my parents to their home. I wanted to be in my own house. Maybe I didn't realize what had happened yet, or maybe I wanted to have the memories of my husband close to me. I'm not sure which it was. So they stayed with me for a while. For a few nights it was both my parents, and then just my mother, and then after a while she left me by myself. They called throughout that first evening when I was alone and the next morning, checking on me, trying to help. Then, after a while, I had a day when I didn't hear from any of them, James's parents or my own. I was alone with my thoughts.

I cried a lot. I cried for a long time. There were times when it was all I could do. You become addicted to it. I just needed to let it out so badly. I'd wake up and reach over and feel for him. I knew he wasn't there. I knew that, but I still moved my hand around in his space, wishing he were beside me, crying because I knew he wasn't.

We made arrangements. We had a service for James, and his mother broke down. She screamed and wept, and his father held on to her while tears ran from the same blue eyes that he had passed on to his son. Somehow I made it. Somehow, with the help of my mom and dad, I managed to get through it.

There was no normal, and I knew there wouldn't be for a long time. He was always in my thoughts. I remembered the way he'd touch my hand, and I thought of our loss and how he'd been there for me when I was in the hospital. And I thought back to our early days at Treshingham, the good ones. Eventually I thought about our last trip there, and although I tried to ignore it, a bit of me still wondered what he'd been trying to say. There were times when I thought maybe he knew something wrong with his heart. Then there were other times when I realized that it must have been something else. I just tried not to think about it.

At the end, the staff from the hospital were very good to me. They knew how bad his heart was, and they couldn't understand why a doctor at some point in his life hadn't recognized that something was wrong. It wasn't their fault. I checked with our family doctor, and James hadn't had a checkup in years. The nurses and doctors at the hospital did everything they could, but James's death seemed to have surprised them as much as it did all of us. The doctor who first led me down the hallway called and asked how I was doing. She still had her stern, medical voice, but she was calling, and she didn't have to. One of the nurses called too, checking in, telling me about calls that had come to the hospital after James passed and people who had been there checking on him.

My father helped me pack up his clothes, along with the things that I didn't want to keep, and some days I felt like I was almost there. I didn't want a new life. I wanted my old life with my husband back, but I had no choice, I had to accept it; and in spite of myself, little pieces of a life without him began to come together. I needed to do something, anything to help me stop thinking about him. The museum told me they'd have me back anytime. My manager was concerned. The kind, old soul attended the funeral and sat in one of the back rows of the church, weeping as James's accomplishments were read. He wanted to make sure I was okay. He told me not to rush things, but he'd love to have me back even if it was only for a few hours. I thought I'd try it. After sequestering myself away, and hiding, I decided to go back to work. I had to rejoin the world at some point and see whether I could handle it, so I did.

As I pulled out of the parking garage of our apartment block, I looked at the street and took in the life that I'd been avoiding. There were cars driving by, people walking. It was all the same, mundane things that always happened. When I drove out into the traffic, a vehicle that looked like it had been parked at the side of the road pulled in behind me. I turned my usual left and then two rights, getting on the highway, and the vehicle stayed behind me. We were two commuters, both traveling in the same direction. It was just one of the things that happened in the real world.

I drove at the speed limit on the highway. I was in no hurry. The same vehicle stayed discreetly behind me. It didn't mean a thing. It was someone else going to the city, perhaps someone from my apartment building, or my neighborhood. When I reached the museum I pulled into the small employee parking lot, took my briefcase from the back seat, and locked my vehicle. I felt okay. I could do this. I was almost there. I was halfway to the front door of the building when I saw him. A soldier dressed in his uniform walked toward me, and behind him I could see the same black jeep that had followed me all the way from my apartment.

I stood my ground and watched him as he marched toward me. I wasn't afraid. He was a large man, but there was a gentleness in his face, a kindness. Then, just as suddenly as he'd started out, he stopped and froze in his tracks. It was like he'd forgotten something. He turned back toward his vehicle as though dismissing me.

"Excuse me."

At first he didn't answer. I followed after him, down the sidewalk, but his pace was too quick. When he looked back his expression was intense, and he seemed puzzled, confused. "Can you stop, please? Please. I can't run. I can't catch you."

And he did. The big man in the uniform turned. His lips were pursed together. It wasn't a smile; it was more of a sadness, and again something told me that I had nothing to fear from him. "I'm sorry. I didn't mean to scare you."

"I'm not afraid. I just wondered what you wanted. Why did you follow me? Do I know you?"

He hesitated, then took a step forward, and put his hand out to shake mine.

"My name is Stephen Brown, and no, we don't know each other. My wife knew your husband. I'm very sorry for your loss."

It was the last piece of the puzzle. It had to be.

"How did she know James? Did they work together?"

He nodded. He was giving me as little as he could.

"I think they may have. I'm sorry to have troubled you. I shouldn't have come here. Again, I'm sorry for your loss."

There was something in his expression, something I recognized but couldn't quite put my finger on. He backed away from me, turning, apologizing again. My hand was still warm from where he shook it. Then, I knew what it was. He was hurting too. That's what I sensed in him. That's what I saw in his face.

"Stephen, is it Sergeant Brown, or Corporal? I don't know how to tell."

His voice was official now and he sounded the way I thought a soldier should sound.

"It's sergeant, ma'am. I'm a sergeant."

"Why don't you let me buy you a coffee, Sergeant? I think you owe me that, don't you?"

He couldn't say no; I knew he wouldn't. I turned and motioned for him to follow me.

"It's okay. It's just over here."

After a moment's hesitation I could hear him walking behind me.

He collected two plain, black coffees for us from the counter of the coffee bar and settled his big frame into the seat across from me.

He kept his eyes on me, but his voice was shaky, and his big hand held on to his coffee cup as though he was trying to find some comfort in it.

"You must know this area. You knew where the coffee shop was."

"It's Seattle, there's a coffee shop on every corner. Aren't you from here?"

He smiled at me, as though realizing his mistake.

"Yes, of course there is. I know that, sorry. I live in Olympia, not far away. I'm staying with my friend right now, Billy Stewart. It's only temporary."

"You're not with your wife? Do you both live at your friend's house?"

His reply came back immediately.

"My wife and I have separated. We're divorcing."

There had been a woman, a face in the glass, crying. I saw her once, but I was too busy attending to my husband, watching the doctors trying to save him in his final minutes. It wasn't important at the time or even afterward. I didn't even think about it until the nurse called and said that a woman who wouldn't give her name had asked questions after we left. She had asked to see James, but they wouldn't let her. When the nurse phoned me, she wanted to know whether I knew her. She assumed the woman was an estranged family member or perhaps even an ex-wife. It was one more piece of the puzzle.

"Tell me what you know, Sergeant. Tell me about your wife and my husband."

He stopped looking at me and stared into his coffee cup. After a while he sighed and looked back up.

"I made a mistake coming here. I shouldn't have, this isn't fair to you. I was angry. I don't get angry very often, and you're the last person who deserves to be hurt right now. I wasn't thinking."

"I'll worry about that. Just tell me. I have a right to know."

He didn't look like he agreed, but he nodded and began to tell me.

"They were having an affair."

I knew. I'd figured it out, but I still gasped. His hand reached for mine, but I shook my head, and he pulled it back. I needed to know more, and I gave him no choice.

"I'm fine. Keep going, please."

"I don't know everything, but it had been going on for some time. My wife works, or at the time, she worked in a supermarket."

The blanks were being filled in.

"Yes, of course she did."

"The two of them struck up a relationship. My sister works there too. We were all at dinner together one night, it was just an innocent meal, and my sister mentioned your husband's name, and said how ill he was. She didn't know about the affair. When my wife heard about his condition she got upset and ran away. I believe she went to the hospital."

The face in the glass.

"I'm sorry. You shouldn't have to deal with this. It isn't fair. I shouldn't have come."

I wanted to know, but I did not want to know. James was going to tell me. That day at Treshingham he almost said it. My good man, James almost confessed. His conscience wouldn't allow him to carry it around any longer. He must have been in so much pain. I could see it in his face, the anguish he was feeling. I wish I could have taken that away from him. It was strange, but I didn't feel any jealousy. I just wished I'd been able to help him a little more. I sat for a while and stared out the window of the coffee shop, thinking about him, missing him. It was a few minutes before I realized there was a soldier sitting across from me, dealing with his own misery.

"What's her name? What's your wife's name?"

"Her name is Myra."

I needed the name, and I thought I'd feel better if I heard it, but I didn't. It made it worse. That's when the anger came, and I had nowhere to put it.

"Has she done this before? Is this what she does to couples, breaks them up?"

I could taste the salt from my tears trickling into the corner of my mouth. I didn't realize I was crying. He tried to reach out once more, but I shook my head again, still pushing him away.

"I don't know. I hope not, but I don't know. She's gone. I guess she's probably been gone for a long time."

The big, kind man was hurting too. There was pain in his eyes. I knew what that looked like, what it felt like.

"You shouldn't have to deal with this either. I'm sorry about your marriage."

"It's fine. She was the wrong girl. My friend Billy tells me that. He says it's really simple. She and I wanted different things. I wanted a family and I thought she did too, but I was wrong. It didn't work out. I guess I picked the wrong girl."

He lay back in his seat a little, as though he felt guilty for sharing his feelings with me.

We sat in our own, respective miseries for a moment. Now that I knew what James had been trying to tell me I didn't know what to do with the information. You make little steps in recovery. You get up in the morning and you dress yourself and shower, and then the next day you manage to make yourself dinner, and you cry your eyes out as you sit and eat alone. Then you build up enough strength and decide to go in to work for a few hours. I'd made it this far. I wasn't going to go backward. I couldn't.

"I should go, ma'am. I'm sorry. I'm sorry about all of it."

I took a handkerchief from my purse and dabbed at my wet eyes. I didn't want to look at him; I just stared at the name stamped on the pocket of his uniform.

He got up from the table and looked at me with a big soulful stare.

"Are you going to be okay?"

I told him the truth.

"I don't know."

He nodded. He had walked all the way to the door before turning around and coming back. My hands were in front of me on the table, and I didn't pull back this time. He put one of his big, kind hands around mine.

"Somebody told me something a long time ago. They said, 'God isn't going to drop you now after bringing you this far.' I've always remembered that. It's helped me get through lots of tough times."

I smiled, believing him and not believing him at the same time.

"Anyway, I just thought I'd let you know, in case it helps."

Then he left. I waited a moment, still wiping the tears from my eyes. I'd suspected, but I wasn't sure. I wanted to know, but I didn't want to know. It was too much to figure out. Maybe when you're hurting this bad all you really want is to be with someone else who's hurting too. So, I went after him. I don't really know why, but I did. He was sitting in his jeep with the engine running, and he rolled down the window when I walked up.

"Where will you go now? What will you do?"

"I'm going back to where things make sense. I received my orders yesterday; I leave for Afghanistan in a few days. I've been there before. It's familiar to me."

I've never known men and women who participate in wars, but I knew enough about them to know that sometimes they don't come back.

"That doesn't make sense. You shouldn't go, Stephen, Sergeant. You don't have to, do you?"

He nodded. His pain was there, just like mine. It wasn't going away.

"Thank you for your concern. I appreciate that. I really do, but I requested it. It's my decision, and I'm going back."

He wasn't rude or brash. He just drove off, wishing me well, and apologizing one last time.

I cried all the way home in the car. When I reached our apartment, my apartment, I turned on the television and adjusted the volume to low. I didn't want to watch it, but I needed to have some sound. I needed something, anything other than the silence, and the emptiness. I flicked past the soap operas and the comedy programs and settled on the news. I sat in my husband's favorite chair, the one where he'd balanced his laptop on his knees as he worked. On the screen it showed images of a story about a senior citizen who was losing his home, and then I watched a tale about a pet that had been rescued. I thought about the times I'd stared at James as he tried to fight the pain that he had inside. I thought about the good times, and the times when we made plans for the future. It wasn't disappointment I'd seen in his face; it had been uncertainty. I thought about his sparkling blue eyes and the way he used to touch my hands. And I thought about the things he'd done that I didn't know about. Then the news showed a battle scene from a war that I'd tried to ignore, and I thought of the soldier who had sat across from me, and driven away, just a few hours earlier.

# Stephen

Billy explained to me that the Internet is the great
equalizer. I'd almost had to bribe the sergeant at Fort Lewis
to give me Billy's address, but with the aid of her
computer, and a few clicks of her mouse, it had taken very
little effort for Becky to track me down. She had my name
and rank, and I'd mentioned Billy's name when we'd sat
together having coffee, and that was enough. With that
little bit of information, she was able to find me, and I was
glad that she did. She was easy to talk to. We spoke on the
phone the night after our first meeting, and she told me she
agreed with what I said. She said she did feel like she was
being looked after, but she also didn't think there was any
point in pushing your luck. She said the same thing that
Ally and Mike and Billy told me. She told me I shouldn't
go. She said that the answers to my questions or whatever it
was I was looking for probably weren't in Afghanistan. We
talked for a long time that first night. She told me that she
was going to focus on the things she loved about her
husband and try to remember him that way. He was a good

man who had made a mistake, and that's what she was choosing to remember.

I liked that she was loyal and was trying to find a way to stay positive. She cried a few times during that first phone conversation, but she was doing the right thing. I knew she was. I just had to find a way to get there myself. Even though I knew Myra and I were finished, I still had anger toward her, and I knew that wasn't healthy. I needed to find a way to forgive her.

Myra hadn't gone back to work at the supermarket, but Allyson told me that the rumor-mill alerted her that she was already dating one of the assistant managers from the store. This time my sister was hearing everything that happened at her workplace whether she wanted to or not. She was the wrong girl for me; I knew that now. We'd married too quickly, and it was my fault as much as hers. She found her way out and took it. Maybe she was in love with Becky's husband or maybe she wasn't. I'll never know. I just had to try to do what my new friend was doing. I'd moved on; and now I had to try to forgive her.

Becky and I spoke every evening leading up to the time I was due to leave. I felt as though I'd known her for a long time. There were moments when it seemed like I was having a conversation with my sister. She did the same things Ally did. She had little conversations with herself, sometimes out loud and sometimes in her head. Then she'd tell you what she had decided. I was familiar with how her mind worked and I told her so, explaining about Allyson. She liked that. She liked that it felt as though we knew each other a little bit already.

When she asked me about Afghanistan I told her about Billy, and his ability to sneak into the darkness, and I told her what happened to us when we sat crouched in a ditch. And I told her how I felt like I'd let him down. She didn't judge. She just listened, and she kept saying the same thing to me. She didn't understand why I was going back.

It was a good way for a friendship to begin, and I was thinking about what she'd said as Billy pulled his jeep outside the main terminal at McChord Air Force Base. There was to be no commercial flight for me this time. I was meeting up with my platoon, and we were flying overseas en masse, back to Afghanistan. I'd almost had to take a bus to the airport. The night before, Billy had told me that if I was hell-bent on going back I could find my own way there, but at the last minute he relented and gave me a long, silent drive to the airport. As he pulled up to the departures terminal he finally spoke.

"You know, you might want to reconsider that whole 'do what I say, not what I do' deal. I was wrong to go over there, Stephen. It didn't solve a thing. You, especially, should know that."

He'd never brought it up. We'd never really talked about our time in the ditch. I looked at my friend's face and remembered the days of darkness he'd experienced. I wondered if that's where I was now. Was that why I'd been so intent on delivering bad news to a grieving widow? Was that why I was going back?

"I know that. It doesn't matter. Nothing matters."

I opened the door and just as I was ready to jump out he reached over and grabbed my arm.

"It does though. I had nobody. You do though, Stephen. You're not thinking this through."

I thought about Ally and Mike and the children, and how my sister couldn't look at me when I went to say goodbye. As I was leaving her home she'd called after me, telling me that Myra knew I was going back overseas and didn't care. She was just like Billy's wife. That was obvious to me now. I heard the boarding call for my flight on the outside speaker, and I thought about how I was letting them down. And I thought about the advice I'd given so freely to my new friend the day I met her at the coffee shop.

She was right. They all were. It wasn't worth it. I wasn't going to run away from anything; I didn't want to live in the darkness. I closed the door of the jeep and settled back into the chair.

"Let's get out of here. I'm not going. Now I just need to figure out a way to tell the army without being courtmartialled."

He smiled and fired the jeep into gear. When he accelerated into the traffic, he cut off a taxicab, and we could hear the angry sounds of the vehicle's horn blasting at us as we sped away from the airport.

## Becky

You learn to accept that the things you thought you always knew were wrong, and the things you thought you'd always have, aren't there anymore. I forgave James. It was easier than I thought it would be. I still had my thoughts about the other woman, and I certainly had my weak moments, but I made a decision. I decided not to question why he did it or what I could have done differently. That would be wasting energy, and I didn't want to do that. The problem I had was revising the memory I had of him. He'd been perfect to all of us. He was the perfect son-in-law to my parents, the perfect son to his parents, and the perfect salesman, but he made a mistake, and he wasn't the perfect husband any more. I had to find a way to hold him in my heart and remember him so that I wouldn't think less of him and our time together. He introduced me to a feeling that I hadn't known existed. The first time that I told him I loved him I felt something inside me that made every other emotion I'd ever experienced feel meaningless. Without him I'd never have known what that felt like. There was nothing like it, and I never thought I'd feel it again.

When Stephen and I became friends, I truly felt that's all we'd be. A soldier can't just refuse an order, especially when it involves reporting to your unit and being deployed overseas. So, when Stephen didn't rejoin his combat unit and travel back to Afghanistan, the army ordered him to take a little mental health break in the military hospital in Tacoma for a few weeks. It was good for him. It helped him get back on his feet, and that's how we got to know each other. His friend Billy gave him a laptop, and while he was under observation we spoke online, through our computers. We'd spoken on the phone a few times before he was due to fly out, so I felt like I knew him a little bit. Online conversations are different though, and our first talks as we typed into our computers were general and polite. After we'd had a few chats, I suppose I began to feel a bit more mischievous, and I thought I'd have some fun with the big, serious soldier.

"So, do you feel like you're nuts? Do the padded walls feel comforting to you?"

There was no response. His usual rapid-fire, polite response did not come. I watched the screen on my computer. I got up and walked to my apartment window and looked out. I came back and stared at the blank screen, waiting for something to come back. Maybe he did need help. He'd been through a lot. I knew he'd been to Afghanistan before, and his relationship with his wife had just ended.

Finally the little bubble popped up and I could read his words.

"Well..."

Yes. Come on. Five and then ten seconds passed and still nothing. I refreshed my screen.

"I did hear Billy telling me he enjoyed chewing Juicy Fruit gum the other day. Maybe I am in the right place. Maybe I'm his Jack Nicholson."

He was crazy, or was I missing something? Did he think he was the movie star? I tried to picture the face I'd seen at the coffee shop. How would it have looked as he typed those words in?

"I don't understand, Stephen. Are you talking about Jack Nicholson, the actor?"

The little message bubble popped up immediately and a smiley face appeared beside it. He was enjoying playing with his computer.

"My friend Billy walks around in here saying that to all of the other patients. The doctors and nurses are tired of hearing it, but all the guys laugh their heads off when he does it."

I laughed even though I still didn't know what I was laughing at, and then I let him experience the pause as I chose not to answer him right away.

"It's from a movie, Becky. My friend Billy is a Native Indian and in the movie, *One Flew Over The Cuckoo's Nest*, there is a patient who's native and at one point he chews Juicy Fruit gum."

"I'm still not with you. Can you reference something from *Sleepless In Seattle* please? Then, I'll know what you're talking about."

"It's a funny scene. Jack Nicholson and the native fellow are sitting together and all of a sudden..."

"Oh, I remember it now. I've seen it."

And I had. I watched it with my Dad. And, they were in a hospital.

"It's classic, absolutely classic. Oh, that's funny. And your friend makes the other patients laugh with his line? That's priceless. I need to meet Billy. I like him already."

"Yes, I think my visit here is helping him more than me. He's here every day, bringing me books, making people laugh. I even saw him flirting with one of the nurses the other day."

I was smiling and I'd been smiling for a while. It felt good, but I felt as though I was doing something wrong.

Sometimes, I thought I could still smell my husband's scent when I walked into our bedroom. There were days when I expected the phone to ring and hear his voice telling me about a deal he'd been working on or see his jacket hung over the back of the door. It didn't feel right to be laughing and smiling and sending messages to another man from my computer. It couldn't be the right thing to do. I typed in a polite goodnight and told my friend that I needed to get some rest. I didn't wait for a response. I just logged off and stared out my apartment window at the streetlights twinkling down below.

He never asked me to explain my hasty goodnights or my quick transformation from polite friend to mischievous girl. Each time we spoke, mischievous girl stayed a little longer, and I found myself looking forward to our online conversations more and more. I delayed my return to work, taking advantage of my kind manager's good nature, and in between Stephen attending his counseling sessions we always found time to talk. Once, in the space of twenty-four hours, he told me about his time in Afghanistan and his sister and her children, and about the tragedy that happened when their parents were killed. And I told him about how James and I lost our baby. It felt like we'd shared the heaviest parts of our lives with each other, and when we spoke of my husband, or even when we spoke of his wife, it was as though we'd all known each other. There was a comfort with him, but it still felt peculiar to be speaking to someone who was one degree of separation away from what had happened. He was feeling it too. I knew that because he addressed it first.

"It's odd, isn't it?"

"Yes, I know."

"We didn't plan it though, Becky."

"I know that. I know we didn't, Stephen."

This time the pause was comfortable, and I knew he'd probably be propped up in his bed, smiling perhaps, staring at his screen.

"They're letting me out tomorrow. Apparently, I'm cured. Billy's picking me up."

I laughed as I typed in my answer to him.

"I thought so. I thought you'd told me it was tomorrow."

I didn't expect him to ask. We'd been sequestered in our own online world for almost a month. We could have spoken on the phone, or I could even have gone to the hospital to visit him, but I didn't. We never spoke about it, but somewhere along the line we'd made a silent pact to only speak through our computers. We'd enjoyed each other's company and the online isolation of it all. I hadn't looked ahead. I had just enjoyed being with him.

"I'd like to see you. Maybe we could hang out if you want to."

He wasn't asking me on a date. We were friends, online friends really. That was all. We laughed, and enjoyed each other's company. If we did meet in person, the comfort level that we had online might not be there, and the friendship we'd built might not carry over. In spite of ourselves, somehow, we'd become friends. It was more than that though—it was a connection. I had to admit that to myself. Stephen and I had made a connection, and whatever that connection was, it might not be there when we actually met in person again. I'd paused too long, and his next message popped up.

"Or, we couldn't. I could message you every night from Billy's and we could keep doing this. I'd be good with that. Really, I would."

I smiled, remembering his kind face.

"I'd like to see you, Stephen. That would be nice. And, I'd like to meet Billy. I have to meet him too."

When I said goodnight to him and shut down my computer, my first thought was that I hoped we'd like each other as much in person as we had online. Then I began to feel guilty again, and wondered how I was supposed to be feeling.

## Stephen

Each time Billy visited me in the hospital he was wearing a different shirt, and each one was a little more stylish and colorful than the one before. And, as time passed, his expression became clearer and less troubled. I truly believe that my hospital visit benefited him more than it did me. I got lots of rest, and of course I had my daily conversations with Becky, but he emerged from his darkness. It was good for him. Visiting me seemed to have given him a purpose. It was after I got out that things changed and he decided to act like he was my older, wiser brother.

"It's not a date though. Or, is it, Stephen? Is that what it is? Because, if it is I can loan you some nice civilian clothes. You know, something that was maybe manufactured this century? That whole grey T-shirt and faded blue jeans look doesn't really work anymore.""Your clothes wouldn't fit me. I'm too big for them."

"Don't be so sure, Sergeant, you've been on hospital food for two weeks, remember."Life can change so quickly. One minute you think you're all set, trying to make things work with your marriage, building a life, and in the next instant you're living with your friend, wondering where you're going next. Life never stops. Even when we think things are standing still they're not. They're still changing; we're just not always aware of the changes.

During our online conversations, when I talked to Becky about my relationship with Myra and what had happened, I did it almost reluctantly because I knew that her situation was far more tragic than mine. During the brief times when I mentioned it, she would tell me that I'd been run over, and it was going to take a while before I felt like I was myself again. She was right. I enjoyed talking to her, and our conversations were seamless. We had no agenda, we just wanted to get to know each other a little more and become better friends.

Although Seattle is one of the busiest and loudest cities in the country, it also has a quiet side. There are areas by the water that make you feel as though you've left the land of tall buildings and crowded sidewalks far behind. That's where we decided to meet. We thought we'd walk along the shoreline and talk. It would be similar to talking online. We wouldn't be looking at each other. We could just take in the scenery and say what was on our minds.

Billy loaned me his jeep for the day, and I parked high above in the parking lot and then walked down a steep set of stairs to the beach. The sun was reflecting on the water. It was cold, but in typical western Washington fashion, even though it was February, there was no snow. I pulled the collar of my jacket tight around my neck as I felt the blustery wind blowing in from the water. I thought I saw her several times among the few people who walked briskly past me, but each face turned away as I reached them. Then, in our prearranged spot, at the last bench before the pier, she was standing, waiting for me. She had her parka fastened tight up to her chin, and her mischievous smile peeked out from her hood. Billy had been right. It didn't feel like I was meeting a friend and going for a walk. This was a date.

"I hope I'm not late. Have you been waiting long? Traffic coming from Olympia was busier than I thought it would be."

We stood a few feet apart, smiling, searching each other's faces, looking for a sign. There was a warmness about her, the same warmness I'd experienced when we'd spoken online.

"You're not. You're right on time. It's good to see you."

I reached my hand out to shake hers, and she shook her head.

"Do you really think that's appropriate, Stephen? After all we've talked about and shared, should we be shaking hands?"

I don't know if she came closer to me or me to her, but it felt good to hold her and hug her. We'd been through something and although we'd experienced it separately, in a way it felt as though we'd been through it together too.

We walked along the shoreline. As we talked, the same feeling of comfort I'd felt from the safety of my computer was back. I'd left my gloves in Billy's jeep, and my hand dangled at my side as our shoulders brushed against each other. When the wind picked up and began to whip on either side of us, she moved closer and gently placed her hand in mine.

I asked her a question, as I nervously stared straight ahead.

"You're cold. Do you want to head back?"

When I looked down at her the corners of her mouth were raised and it was there again—the same beautiful smile that had been peeking out from the hood of her parka. Her mischievous voice answered me right away.

"No, and no."

"I don't understand. What does 'no and no' mean, Becky?"

She paused for a moment, and we kept walking, while I held her lovely, soft hand in mine.

"No, I don't want to go back. And, no, I'm not cold. I have my gloves in my pocket. That wasn't why I took your hand."

Her head turned toward me, and I nervously looked away, watching the line of benches in front of us. I felt as though I'd been smiling ever since I'd seen her standing by the water. It was good. It was all good. I didn't kiss her that day and maybe I should have, but something more important happened. She taught me something when she took my hand. By making that simple gesture, after all she'd been through, she told me that you can believe again. You really can. It doesn't matter what's happened or what you've lost—you can believe in your dreams once more. If she could do it, I certainly could. I squeezed her hand a little, and she moved closer to me as we continued walking. I didn't know where Becky and I were headed or how we were going to get there, but all of a sudden, I knew it was possible. I believed, and I knew I could try again.

## Becky

Things became almost normal. It was like a different type of normal. I'd hang out with Stephen and Billy or visit with his sister and her family. Initially, even though we held hands and brushed up against each other from time to time, there was nothing romantic happening with us. There really wasn't. His family and Billy must have thought us a strange pair, but anyone who was around us saw that we were anything but bitter. We didn't commiserate with each other. It wasn't like that. We were survivors, and even though we'd gone through a tough situation, each on the other side of it, we'd survived, and we didn't intend to sit around ruminating about our pain. We made a decision to live.

The first time we kissed it was an accident. We were at Billy's washing his stupid, prized jeep. I'd brought my usual pack of Juicy Fruit gum for him and left it by his front door. It was a running joke with us. I'd ask him if he was still nuts, and before he could answer I'd hand him the package of gum. He was skulking, watching Stephen and I, the way he sometimes did.

"Don't be sneaking around the side of the house there, Billy. Grab a wash brush and help us clean off your little toy."

Just as he started to make a smart remark back to me, Stephen and I reached down for the hose at the same time. As we pulled up, each of us apologized, and our faces touched, and somehow our lips met. And they stayed met. He kissed me. Or I kissed him. I'm not sure which. Billy couldn't resist. He had to say something.

"Finally. Now the skies can open up. Finally, it happens."

I didn't know what to do and neither did Stephen. I could tell. At first he had a sheepish expression on his face, like he'd been caught with his hand in the candy jar. He naturally had a little-boy look about him, but this was a little-boy-guilt look and it was irresistible. He called out to Billy but kept looking at me.

"Do you have to always be sneaking around? It's not nice to spy on people, Billy.""I'm not sneaking. I'm standing right here, washing my truck with both of you, or I thought we were. Now, are the two of you just going to stand there grinning at each other, or are you going to say something?"

I answered him without taking my gaze from Stephen.

"Turn away, Billy."

"I'm sorry, Becky. What are you asking me to do in my own driveway in front of my own jeep?"

"Turn away, invisible man. Show us how stealthy you can be."

He was so happy. He laughed and muttered something to himself, as he headed off toward the front door of his house.

Stephen couldn't stop smiling. Even when he spoke his smile was engrained in his face. He just couldn't help himself.

"Why did you do that? Don't you want him here?"

I moved closer, reached up, and put my lips on his one more time. This time on purpose. Then, for just a moment, something happened. I felt it, and I remembered what it used to feel like. That's when I began to cry.

"Becky, you're crying. What's wrong? Do you want to stop?"

I didn't though. I wanted more, and I knew that even after everything that had happened I was going to be okay. I held on to him, and then kissed him, and then held tight to him again. It was back. The feeling I'd once had, the feeling that I hadn't known I needed was back in my heart. All of a sudden, I knew I wanted the same things I'd wanted all those years ago. And now I thought that maybe I could do it all again.


Eighteen months later, Seattle had a huge snowfall. It was a December for the record books. Snowploughs patrolled the streets, sweeping piles of snow to the edges of the roads, walling us in. Our daughter, Margaret Allyson Brown, was born in the middle of a snowstorm on December twelfth. She was our Christmas baby. Neither my husband Stephen nor I like hospitals, so we made it through the snow and took her home right away. We had lots of help waiting for us. Even before we moved into the house across the street from Stephen's sister, and even before our little Margaret was born, his niece and nephew volunteered to be babysitters. We told them that their Uncle Billy was our first choice if we ever needed a babysitter, but in a few years they'd be able to help too. They liked that. They were good kids and it was going to be nice having them close, looking out for our daughter.

I found something I was good at. I felt as though I was born to be a mother. Where Ally's demeanor was loud and boisterous, I tried to be quiet and calm. We both achieved the same things, and we each love our children; we just approach it differently. I know that it's amusing sometimes for Mike and Stephen to watch us. We're like one large, extended family. There's Stephen and myself, and Allyson and Mike and the kids, and Billy too, of course. Billy never needs an invite. When he first held our daughter, he whispered in her ear that he saw her parents having their first kiss. I teased him and told him that he shouldn't have been sneaking around, but he just smiled and reminded me that he'd seen everything.

I'm sure that over time we'll have a rut in the road from the path we walk across the street, between our two houses. If we're not in one home, we're in the other. It doesn't matter though. It's all the same. Stephen and I had a moment alone on Christmas Eve. We were standing in our living room, watching the snow accumulate outside. Our Christmas tree was twinkling, and when I looked across the street I could see Allyson and Mike waving to us, standing in front of their tree at their front window. Margaret was asleep in her crib, and Billy was dozing on our couch. Occasionally, he'd snore, and then, just as it seemed as though he was going to wake himself up, he'd fall back to sleep and settle into a peaceful slumber. I snorted and tried not to laugh.

"I'm sorry, it's funny. I keep thinking he's going to wake himself up. Maybe I should put another blanket over him. We don't want him to be uncomfortable. If he has a good sleep maybe he'll make Christmas breakfast for us."

Stephen put his arms around me from behind, and I pushed myself against him, enjoying our familiar position.

"Aha, that's very good thinking. Or maybe, he can watch over Margaret and I can have a few extra moments with my lovely wife."

Sometimes when I'm with him it's as though this feeling in my heart takes me to a different place. He holds on to me, and I know he's feeling the same thing, and all of a sudden, we're not here; we're not anywhere. We're just together, wanting the same things, believing in the same things, and it's like none of the bad things ever happened. I looked up at my husband, gave him a long, loving smile, and explained to him why his idea wouldn't work.

"But, my darling, we'd miss out on having our daughter in bed with us. And, I do know how much you love that."

I was right. He knew I was right. He used to talk about the darkness, but we'd gotten through that. We'd decided to start believing again. We all had, even Billy. It had taken some time, but we got there, and now we were ready to stand in the light and enjoy every minute of it. Stephen believed that he'd get what he wanted and he did. It all came true. We had the right family, together, and like he said to me back when we first met, God didn't bring us this far to drop us now. He hadn't, and he wouldn't. He kissed me gently on the lips, and after peeking in our daughter's door and checking on her, we went to our bed. Christmas Day was a few hours away, and although my life had changed so much and was so different from what I'd imagined, I had what I wanted. I had everything. As the light glistened off the snow and poked through the blinds on our bedroom window, we climbed under our blankets. After a moment, my husband snuggled in beside me, and I felt it. I felt all of it. I was grateful for him, grateful for our life, and grateful that I'd decided to believe again.

# ACKNOWLEDGEMENTS

This story would not have been told without the kind assistance of Tellulah Darling and Mary Anne Lewis. Bethany Gould has always dropped everything and taken the time to help me with my books, and Alyssa Mehl's guidance was incredibly important in making sure I got the facts right. Sable Hunter is a tireless supporter of my work. She and her team worked hard, helping me add some essential elements to this story and for that I'm extremely grateful.

And Pamela Tagle is my secret weapon. Without her, this book would have remained just an idea in my head.

Laurie Boris is the best editor out there. She helps me turn a bunch of words into a readable story.

Thank you all for your help!

**Thanks for purchasing *Believing Again: A Tale of two Christmases*. I hope you enjoyed it!**

In a press release, Amazon referred to Martin Crosbie as one of their success stories of 2012. His self-publishing journey has been chronicled in Publisher's Weekly, Forbes Online, and Canada's Globe and Mail newspaper. Martin's debut novel, *My Temporary Life*, has been downloaded over one hundred and fifty thousand times and became an Amazon bestseller. He is also the author of:

*My Name Is Hardly-Book Two of the My Temporary Life Trilogy*
*Lies I Never Told-A Collection of Short Stories*
*How I Sold 30,000 eBooks on Amazon's Kindle-An Easy-To-Follow Self-Publishing Guidebook 2014 Edition*

Martin was born in the Highlands of Scotland and currently makes his home on the west coast of Canada.

Twitter https://twitter.com/Martinthewriter
Facebook
https://www.facebook.com/martin.crosbie.3
Martin's website http://martincrosbie.com/
Martin's email address
martin@martincrosbie.com
Amazon Author Page
http://tinyurl.com/la5t9eg

**Martin's self-publishing journey has been documented here:**
Publisher's Weekly Apr/2012
**http://tinyurl.com/cq9ygdd**
Globe and Mail newspaper Apr/2012
**http://tinyurl.com/ks2v2e7**
Forbes Online Aug/2012
**http://tinyurl.com/k4v3pnu**

**Martin is a proud contributor at Indies Unlimited:**
http://www.indiesunlimited.com/author/martin-crosbie/

**And, an occasional contributor to the Georgia Straight newspaper:**
http://www.straight.com/user/40034

**Martin's Books:**

**My Temporary Life-Book One of the My Temporary Life Trilogy**

Published Dec. 19, 2011
Publisher-Martin Crosbie
Romantic Suspense
Available on Kindle
Amazon US **http://tinyurl.com/l9xshv6**
Amazon UK **http://tinyurl.com/mxaxtlm**
Amazon Canada **http://tinyurl.com/lgpycef**
Malcolm Wilson learns that everything is always temporary. Growing up, he's raised by a promiscuous mother who can't stay out of trouble, his best friend is a thirteen-year-old alcoholic, and the masters at his tough Scottish school are always raising their canes in his direction. When he becomes an adult, he escapes, and chooses the safe route, watching the rest of the world from a distance. Everything changes the day he meets the beautiful, alluring, green-haired Heather, and when he learns of Heather's own abusive childhood and the horrific secret she's been carrying, Malcolm makes a decision-this time he's not backing down, whatever the cost.

The first book of the MY TEMPORARY LIFE Trilogy deals with friendship, love, and what it means to be a hero. It was a top-ten Amazon bestseller in all categories.

**What readers are saying about *My Temporary Life:***

*There were moments of magic, scenes filled with foreboding, passages that were poetic and ruminative, others that were breathtaking. The masterful handling of Malcolm's mother, was brilliant. There were many scenes, especially toward the end, that were fast-paced and made the book impossible to put down.*

**Susan Russo Anderson-Amazon review**

*I have to say I have not read a book that took me on such an emotional ride in many years. I just finished it and I'm still reeling. I am typically a romance/fantasy reader but this is definitely going on my favorite books list. Martin Crosbie will be on my watch list of authors in the future. This was an incredible story to read.*

**Patricia Paonessa-Goodreads review**

*Mr. Crosbie's first novel is a wonder! Once I started, I couldn't stop. I just HAD to find out what happened next. His characters are so believable and I felt a real connection to his hero's kind heart and the difficulties he faced while growing up and throughout his life. I completed the novel in just a day and was sad to have it end.*

**My Name Is Hardly-Book Two of the My Temporary Life Trilogy**

Published Dec. 10/2012
Publisher-Martin Crosbie
Historical Fiction
Available on Kindle
Amazon US **http://tinyurl.com/jw7mf72**
Amazon UK **http://tinyurl.com/lkr3w3u**
Amazon Canada **http://tinyurl.com/n8hmu6u**
A beautiful girl is missing, and may or may not want to be found, a soldier on his last and most dangerous mission, and a vow made to a dying friend. Northern Ireland, in 1996, was one of the most dangerous places in the world. The government called it a state of unrest, the people who lived through it called it the time of "The Troubles".

Gerald "Hardly" McDougall is a forgotten man. He's abused, bullied, and left behind. The only escape left is to join the British Army. At first, he's a reluctant soldier, then everything changes when tensions in Northern Ireland escalate and the Army need a man with a particular set of characteristics. Hardly's re-assigned and sent into the heart of the troubles, living in the same houses as the IRA soldiers he's fighting against.

MY NAME IS HARDLY takes the reader on a twenty year journey through Hardly's life--from the beginning, when he leaves Scotland and joins the Army, to the tragic final days when his time as a spy in Ireland has to come to an end.

**What readers are saying about *My Name Is Hardly:***

*Martin Crosbie's remarkable storytelling talent is apparent throughout his most recent novel, "My Name Is Hardly." The story seized me from the first paragraph and held me relentlessly until I'd come to the novel's thoughtful and moving conclusion.*

**Kathleen Lourde-Amazon review**

*I have no doubt that when the last piece is in place, Crosbie's work will stand tall as exemplary literary fiction, and a reproach to those who mourn the decline of the "gatekeepers" of commercial publishing. Any gate too small to let in Martin Crosbie should have been blown up a long time ago.*

# Steven Hart-Goodreads review

## Lies I Never Told-A Collection of Short Stories

Published April 13, 2013
Publisher-Martin Crosbie
Short Story Collection
Available on Kindle
Amazon US **http://tinyurl.com/q7w7vu3**
Amazon UK **http://tinyurl.com/l3ksbky**
Amazon Canada **http://tinyurl.com/mvew4r6**
"It's what we do. We make our own beds. We become thirty and then forty and we divorce and re-marry and visit our children on weekends, and work at jobs we never dreamed of doing, and have too many relationships with people we don't like, and on the outside we look like any other forty-year-old hero. We're not though, because it never goes away. No matter how hard we try to hide it, inside we're still seventeen, sitting at the river, looking for the girl with the brown eyes."

In this collection of short stories, Martin Crosbie, the bestselling author of "My Temporary Life", presents us with a glimpse into the rear-view mirror of life. Crosbie's writing is quiet, so quiet that when the crash comes you suddenly realize you've been gripping onto the edge of your chair, living the story right along with the main character. In this intensely personal collection, he writes about relationships, sex, children, infidelities, guilt, and sometimes, the absence of guilt. *Lies I Never Told* includes four new, original stories, one previously published short story, and the first chapters of his Amazon bestselling novel *My Temporary Life* and the follow-up *My Name Is Hardly*.

**What readers are saying about *Lies I Never Told-A Collection of Short Stories*:**

*Could not put this book down. I am amazed at the depth of feeling and emotion in his words. All of the stories are so different yet so connected at the emotional level. My only disappointment is that the stories were not longer. I really hope that this book is just a prelude of the novels to come. Martin grabs me from the first line and takes me on an emotional journey with all his characters.*

**Debbie Dore-Amazon review**

*Where Martin Crosbie found his voice is a mystery. His ability to create stories (here very brief ones) that explore the psyche of his chosen stand-in trope in such a way that within a few sentences you are so aware of the character's life and feelings that he seems to be sitting beside you, in conversation with only you.*

**Grady Harp (Hall of Fame reviewer)-**
**Goodreads review**

**How I Sold 30,000 eBooks on Amazon's Kindle-An Easy-To-Follow Self-Publishing Guidebook**

Published Sept. 4, 2013
Publisher-Martin Crosbie
Self-Help-Sales and Marketing
   Amazon US **http://tinyurl.com/ppxud2p**
   Amazon UK **http://tinyurl.com/ne7jnmc**
   Amazon Canada **http://tinyurl.com/ozf24m3**

- Outlines the methods that the top 5% of successful self-published authors utilize to produce their eBooks in a professional, cost-effective manner
- Shows what happened after Amazon changed the rules and what you need to do right now to adjust your strategy
- How to adopt the philosophy that will allow promotional opportunities to come to you
- What you need to know in order to position yourself for a run at the bestseller lists

In February 2012 Martin Crosbie's self-published eBook *My Temporary Life* hit Amazon's top ten overall bestseller list. The next month Amazon posted a press release revealing that Crosbie had made $46,000 in one month, with one book. Previously to this, his novel was rejected one hundred and thirty times by traditional publishers and agents.

In the months that followed, *My Temporary Life* and its sequel have been consistent sellers, often sitting atop Amazon's rankings. Crosbie's story has been mentioned in *Publisher's Weekly*, *Forbes online*, and other media outlets around the world. In fact, Amazon referred to him as one of their 2012 success stories in their year-end press release. *How I Sold 30,000 eBooks on Amazon's Kindle-An Easy-To-Follow Self-Publishing Guidebook* tells the story of how he became a full-time writer, detailing the specific steps he took to find and connect with his readers. Plus, it describes how to adjust and tweak your strategy as Amazon changes their systems.

**What readers are saying about *How I Sold 30,000 eBooks on Amazon's Kindle-An Easy-To-Follow Self-Publishing Guidebook*:**

*Yes, I was skeptical because I've read one or two of these books, and their suggestions are... let's just say not that good. Last night, I skipped* the intro and jumped right to the meat of the book. Chapter One was better, much better, than I had expected. But it was when he said, DON'T go out on Twitter and FB and shout "read my book" a thousand times a day that he convinced me that he was honest and knew what he was talking about.

For anyone at the publishing stage or who wants to get there, so far :-) [I will always be a hardcore skeptic] this is a good reference on what to do, on how to build relationships instead of walls. If you're not yet at the publishing stage, start now to build an audience and support group. And Martin C practices what he preaches, especially the part about supporting other authors. He followed me back on Twitter and friended me on FB.

**NSW-Amazon Review**

If you are a new writer this book is a must. I wish I had it when I first started writing. It is filled with easy to read and easy to understand information. However, even if you are an already published writer this book will offer you new information you might not have known. I found it helpful in so many ways. There are also links to various other sites that offer valuable info that is very difficult to find. Basically, "How I Sold 30,000

*Ebooks on Amazon Kindle," takes a lot of the guessing and hard work out of self publishing.*
**Roberta Kagan-Amazon Review**

**I'd love to connect with you!**

https://twitter.com/Martinthewriter
https://www.facebook.com/martin.crosbie.3
http://martincrosbie.com/
martin@martincrosbie.com


### ###

CPSIA information can be obtained
at www.ICGtesting.com
Printed in the USA
LVOW01s1752070416
482606LV00019B/919/P